Crescent River

Karen Rogers

 FriesenPress

One Printers Way
Altona, MB R0G 0B0
Canada

www.friesenpress.com

Copyright © 2023 by Karen Rogers
First Edition — 2023

All rights reserved.

No part of this publication may be reproduced in any form, or by any means, electronic or mechanical, including photocopying, recording, or any information browsing, storage, or retrieval system, without permission in writing from FriesenPress.

ISBN
978-1-03-917342-2 (Hardcover)
978-1-03-917341-5 (Paperback)
978-1-03-917343-9 (eBook)

1. FICTION, CHRISTIAN, ROMANCE, SUSPENSE

Distributed to the trade by The Ingram Book Company

Crescent River

Crescent River

Spring flowers of red, purple, and white arrayed the hills of Crescent River; a carpet of green grass completed the quilt of beauty. The air was fresh and clean after a recent rain. Overhead, the azure sky, made brilliant by the brightness of the sun, lent an atmosphere of tranquility.

Down on the plains by the banks of the river, people were arriving to celebrate spring with a church picnic. Fires lit in fire pits crackled with the burning of wood and wisps of smoke spiraled up to the heavens above while children, playing, laughing, and running around, captured the joy of the day.

George and his friend Scott arrived together in George's 1969 Camaro SS. George had spent two years rebuilding this classic car. The boys climbed out of the car, gathered their food out of the trunk, along with a couple of lawn chairs, and went in search of George's parents.

After locating his parents and dropping off the food, George and Scott decided to go down to the river to see if anyone was fishing. As they were walking along the meandering path beneath tall pines, they could hear laughter and shrieking. Breaking into a run, they raced each other through the trees before stopping dead in their tracks on the edge of the high riverbank. There, wading in the river, were girls—lots of girls. They were dressed in T-shirts and shorts or in sundresses, laughing, and splashing each other—just enjoying themselves.

A girl spying the boys waved hello. Others looked up but went back to having fun. George, the tallest of the two, at age eighteen, stood six feet four inches. With his dark skin, curly black hair, and well-muscled body, he was considered quite handsome, but it was his warm, friendly smile that brought him close to people. George never considered himself any better looking than anyone else, but his confidence was what made people like and trust him.

Suddenly, one of the girls slipped and fell into the water. When another girl tried to help her up, she landed in the water as well. Soon all the girls were falling in the water, laughing even harder. George immediately started shouting and raced down to the edge of the water. Scott joined him and they waved their arms, beckoning the girls to get out of the water. Mistaking their actions, the girls merely thought the boys were making fun of them until one of them looked around and saw their danger. She screamed and made for the shore. Panic gripped all the girls. Laughter changed to screams of terror, for in the water, coming straight toward them, was the river monster—*le diable de la rivière*, the River Devil.

The gigantic monster was about twenty to twenty-five feet from snout to tail tip. It weighed in at two thousand pounds. Even though sharply ridged armored scales covered its entire body, the monster slid incredibly gracefully through the water. Swimming swiftly toward its prey, its humongous mouth opened wide, showing two rows for razor-sharp teeth, which were about to bite down on an unfortunate girl whose foot was caught in a tangle of weeds. At the sight, George dove into the water and helped the girl free her foot. She frantically swam to shore, arriving just in time to hear the snapping of the monster's mouth closing behind her. She crawled higher up the riverbank and fainted.

George swam underwater for a few feet and climbed out of the river, a few feet from where the river monster slipped underwater. Adrenalin coursed through his veins as he rushed up to where the girl had fainted. She was coming around as one of her friends rubbed and patted her hands.

"Wake up, Harriett! You are safe now," encouraged her friend. "Come on, wake up!"

Harriett opened her eyes just as George knelt beside her. "What happened?" asked Harriett as she struggled to sit up.

"You were caught in some weeds and were about to become that old river monster's lunch," explained her friend as she helped Harriett to her feet. "If it were not for this guy, you would not be here. God must have something special in mind for you."

Harriett looked at her rescuer and said, "Thank you for saving my life. I do not know what I can ever do to repay you."

"Well, you could marry me," blurted out George. George blushed and wondered where that had come from. All he knew was that he could not take his eyes off her; all he saw was the most gorgeous girl he had ever laid eyes on.

Harriett looked at him, laughed, and said, "You have made my day. First by saving my life and second by offering me your hand in marriage. By the way, what is your name?"

The laughter and reassurance that she was okay, calmed Harriett. She started walking back to the picnic grounds. All the other girls had already drifted back. Harriett walked between her friend and George. Scott brought up the rear.

"My name is George Hamer. I come from Hidden Valley. My folks and I are visiting some friends here, and they invited us to this picnic. This is my friend Scott." George glanced back at his friend, who was smirking and winking at him. George shot a look at him and shook his head, determined to ignore him.

"I don't know your name either," said George, looking straight ahead.

"Oh my, yes, of course, you should know my name seeing as how you rescued me. My name is Harriett Evelyn Baird," replied Harriett, "and I live here in Crescent River. Oh look, here comes my dad! Thanks again, George!" Harriett ran into her father's arms. He hugged his daughter, smiled at George, and said thanks. He kept his arm around Harriett and led her away.

George and Scott stopped at the edge of the picnic grounds. George bolted to his left and proceeded to his car.

"Hey, George!" called Scott. "Aren't we going to have lunch?"

"No, not hungry. Going for a drive. You go eat and enjoy yourself. I will catch up to you later," replied George as he came to his car, then got in, fired up the Camaro, and pulled out.

George had worked hard for his car. He had worked on various farms and ranches after school, on weekends, and all through several summers. As he worked, he dreamed of restoring his 1969 Camaro SS. This one had a 350 engine, with a four-barrel carburetor, and a four-speed transmission, with four-on-the-floor stick shift. The car was pure muscle. A black vinyl roof and the body painted midnight blue, with the interior finished in black and the seats covered with black-and-white houndstooth fabric brought this Camaro back to its former glory.

Usually when George was in his car, he took time to notice the fine details of the interior. He would listen to the roar of the engine and take great pleasure in it. But not today. Not this moment. He could not get his mind off the morning events or off Harriett.

"How could I be so stupid as to ask her to marry me! What a dork! What a jerk! What an ultra moron! 'Well, you could marry me,'" he lamented in a sarcastic tone out loud. "How could I have said such a stupid thing to her! Oh, what a dolt I am!" With that, he banged his hand against the steering wheel.

Just then a doe and her fawn darted out of the trees and onto the road. Startled, George hit the brakes and swerved to miss the deer. The car sped passed the deer with screeching brakes and fishtailed several yards before George finally came to a stop on the shoulder of the road. Shaking George opened his door and stepped out of the car. His knees were shaking so violently that he collapsed to the ground and began to heave up what he had eaten for the last four days—at least, that was what it looked like to him.

An old pick-up truck pulled in behind George, and an elderly man got out and approached him.

"Hey, son, looks like you are having a bad time of it. I have been following behind you for quite a spell. You handled that situation with the deer very well, but might have been better had you not been going so fast," said the stranger.

George looked up at the elderly man and was surprised to see that he was taller than him. The stranger stood ramrod straight, and his white hair came down over his ears. His clear blue green eyes were fastened on George. The man seemed old but young at the same time, and there was authority about him. George sensed great compassion in him.

"Yeah, well, I guess you are right. I do not know why I am feeling this way. I am supposed to be strong; I am a man after all. But right now, I feel like a foolish little boy," said George contritely.

The elderly man laughed; a big booming laugh that came from deep within. George became very annoyed and started to get back in his car.

"Hang on there a second, son," said the man as he put a large hand on George's arm.

George was about to shake it off his arm in anger when he suddenly felt his anger dissipate and saw the humor in what he said. "I guess I am a fool and feeling sorry for myself."

"Aw, don't be so hard on yourself, son," said the man. "When one has been through what you have, we say and think silly things. Adrenalin does that. Now you have had two scares and the body reacts. You see, we are designed that way for self-preservation. We are not built to take too many hits like that, though. You should have taken the time to rest and eat some lunch. Then you would have been ready for the next incident."

George considered what the old man was saying, and it occurred to him that this man knew about what happened at the river. But George did not remember seeing him at the picnic grounds or at the river. George was sure that he would have remembered because this man was not someone who would go unnoticed. George turned his head to look directly at the old man, but the man had turned so that he stood next to George, facing the road.

George studied his profile before asking, "How do you know what happened this morning?"

The old man stared straight ahead and said, "I was there, at least not too far away. I watched you. You did not hesitate to dive in to save that young girl. That was very brave of you. You did everything right."

George reviewed the morning events in his head and realized that he could have been killed himself, as these river monsters were known travel in pairs. Where was the other one?

It was as if the old man could read George's mind: "The other river monster has since died. This one, too, will die, because without two, it cannot survive on its own. This one will either die from starvation or someone will kill it. The river will once again flourish with life as it is supposed to. Man does not understand that certain creatures were made for certain locations, and when the ecosystem is upset, it messes everything up."

"To be honest with you, I agree, but I will be so glad when this one to dies and the river returns to normal. It has been hard on Hidden Valley, as this river feeds into our river, and without fish or very few fish and other crustaceans, our fishing industry has suffered. Also, without the natural creatures in our waters, our water has become very dirty and almost unfit to drink."

The old man nodded his head in agreement. Then he said, "Well, son, I must head out. Take care. Oh, one last thing . . . do not take your life for granted and be ready and willing to make changes as they come." The old man got back into his truck, turned around, and went back the way he had come.

Chapter 1

George was in his fourth year of university, and he was looking forward to working this summer for one of the top engineering firms in the country, in Orion City. George was excited; the company had promised to underwrite his last year of university. How could it be that a boy from the mountains could obtain such things? Life was good! He decided to head out with the guys to celebrate.

George did not really like to drink but did consent to have a beer with his friend Scott and the guys. That night, a fellow who was not part of George's usual crowd had invited himself to join George and his friends. George took an instant dislike to him. The fellow had a crafty look to his ferret like face and seemed to have a perpetual sneer embedded on his lips. So after a couple of swallows of beer, George excused himself, got up, and left for home.

When George arrived home and unlocked his door, he realized that he was sweating profusely and began shivering violently. He went to lie down on his couch, wondering what he had eaten recently that did not agree with him and hoping he was not getting the flu. Once on his couch, George heard a knock on the door but could not get up to answer it—his world suddenly turned black.

***

"Hey, George, are you okay? I did not even see you leave. Where are you, bud?" called Scott as he
   jiggled the door knob and realized, thankfully, George had not locked his door. He opened the door ran in and found George

passed out on the couch. Scott quickly pulled out his phone and called for an ambulance. He paced the floor, praying that they would arrive in time.

Once the EMTs entered the apartment, Scott explained to them, "There was a new guy in our group tonight who admitted to spiking George's beer with MDMA. That is why I rushed over here to check on him. I arrived, and he was like this. . . . Is George going to be all right? He does not really drink, but tonight, he only had one or two beers. Never takes any kind of drugs, not even an aspirin."

As one of the EMTs quickly inserted an intravenous, the other hooked George up to the heart monitor and thanked Scott for the information he provided. Then they loaded George onto the gurney and wheeled him down to the ambulance, put him in the back, and headed for the hospital with lights flashing and siren blaring. Scott locked up George's apartment and followed them.

When he arrived at the hospital, he sat out in the waiting area. A nurse had come out and asked, "Is there a Scott McDonald here?"

"I'm Scott McDonald."

"Come with me, Mr. McDonald," said the nurse, and she led him to the curtained cubicle where his best friend lay.

Scott could hardly believe his eyes. There lays George with wires attached to his chest, IVs in both his arms, and a breathing tube up his nose.

The emergency room doctor entered the room and asked, "Are you Scott McDonald?"

"Yes, I am."

"Your friend is not in good shape. We have taken bloodwork to try and identify exactly what he took," explained the doctor. "Does George do drugs often?"

"George never does drugs! He is a health nut. He eats properly and exercises regularly. George does not even take an aspirin!" explained Scott, a little irritably.

"I'm just verifying the information given," said the doctor. "Do you know if he has any allergies?"

"Not that I am aware of. You have no idea what this man means to me," said Scott. "George and I have been best friends since kindergarten. Will George wake up?"

"We're doing all we can," said the doctor. "He has come extremely close to death." The doctor went over to the nurse's station, and Scott pulled up a chair and sat next to George.

"Hey, buddy, don't you die on me, man," he said quietly. "God has big plans for you." Scott bowed his head in prayer while he gripped George's hand in his own.

"The report confirms what you said was given to him," the doctor said as he walked back into the room. "Now all we can do is wait and see what happens over the next few hours."

Scott suddenly heard excitement coming from the next cubicle. Through a gape in the curtains, he could see an Evangelist ministering to a teenage boy, who, the minister stated, was the victim of a terrible car accident. Scott could see the patient was badly injured and was in a coma with severe head injuries. If the minister was there, he likely had next to no hope of survival.

The Evangelist asked everyone, including the mother, to leave the cubicle. He then took some anointing oil and placed it on the teenager's head, took hold of the boy's hand, and prayed. "Lord in Heaven, you know this young boy. You know the plans you have for him. This boy is too young to die. Lead me, Lord, in the complete healing and restoration of the boy's life."

The Evangelist bowed his head and waited a moment for the Word of God to be revealed in his spirit. The anointing of healing enveloped the Evangelist.

"Charlie Smith, in the name of Jesus Christ of Nazareth, BE HEALED! WAKE UP, CHARLIE! RECEIVE YOUR HEALING AND RESTORATION NOW!" called out the Evangelist. He continued to pray in his spirit language.

Scott noticed the boy's hand moved in the Evangelist's hand. Then his eyes opened and he met the gaze of the Evangelist.

"Where's my mom?" the boy asked.

His mother and father heard their son's voice and came into the cubicle. Tears of joy and relief flooded his mother's eyes. She quickly gave her son a hug.

His dad, equally charged with emotion, said, "Hey there, boy. You gave us quite a scare. How are you feeling?"

"I am fine. Can we go home now?" answered the boy.

George's heart monitor started beeping loudly, returning Scott's focus to his friend, and causing the doctor and nurses to rush back into his room. They pushed Scott into the hallway and tried in vain to resuscitate George, but to no avail. Minutes later, George was declared dead.

A young nurse, visibly upset, came out of the cubicle, the doctor following behind her. The doctor looked at Scott with sadness and said, "I am sorry, son. We did everything we could. You can stay with him for a while to say your goodbyes."

Scott slowly walked back into the cubicle, sat on the edge of the bed, and looked onto George's peaceful face. Tears of grief slid down Scott's face.

Just then the Evangelist poked his head inside and said quietly, "May I come in?"

Scott turned to face him and nodded his head.

"The Lord spoke into my spirit to stop here. What happened to this young man?" asked the Evangelist.

Scott told him the story, leaving out no details. The Evangelist listened intently as Scott spoke. He closed his eyes for a moment after Scott stopped speaking.

"Do you believe in miracles?" asked the Evangelist.

"Well, I've never really seen one, except when George saved a girl's life," replied Scott.

The Evangelist moved to the head of the bed and laid his hands on George's head. The Evangelist prayed quietly in the Spirit. Then in a loud powerful voice, he said, "In the name of Jesus Christ, George, I command you to come back and wake up NOW!" Again, the Evangelist prayed quietly in the Spirit. Then once more, in a loud and powerful voice, he said, "George, your time has not yet come. WAKE UP in the name of Jesus Christ!"

As the Evangelist said this, George's eyes popped open and he spoke. "What a dream I had! Oh, Scott, what are you doing here? Where am I anyway?"

Scott looked around in time to see the doctor and nurses once again converge on the cubicle. The heart monitor, which had not yet been removed, was showing good, strong heart beats. Everyone began talking at once.

Amazement and wonder filled everyone in the room. Scott did not notice that the Evangelist had left but did recall hearing him say that no one dies until they are ready to depart from this life. He had seen his very first up-close and personal miracle.

Chapter 2

A year after the miracle, Scott completed his fifth year of university, graduating with honors, and soon began his full-time employment with Telstar Engineering Group. One day, as Scott was heading to the lab where he was working, an intern student walked by him and shoved a flyer into his hand. Scott looked at it. It was a well-done glossy-print flyer asking anyone interested in saving planet Earth to attend a rally at Saberly Hall, on the University campus, at seven o'clock that evening. The flyer named the guest speaker: Dr. J. Hilitz, environmentalist and civil rights activist. Scott was interested to hear this man and decided to attend.

Later, at suppertime, Scott took the flyer out of his pocket and handed it to George. He and George had moved into a two-bedroom apartment at the beginning of the school year.

"Thought I might check it out. Want to go?"

"Not tonight. I have a huge project I must work on. I am going back to the lab tonight to get everything organized for tomorrow's meeting. So, knock yourself out and let me know how it goes."

Scott arrived at Saberly Hall at six thirty. The hall was already jammed packed. Scott found a place to stand against the wall near the entrance doors.

"Have you heard this speaker before?" asked a soft voice beside Scott.

Scott looked down to see a petite blond, blued-eyed girl looking up at him. "Ah, no, I have not. Have you?"

"Oh yes, he is a very good speaker. Very knowledgeable," replied the girl. "Do you mind if I stand next to you, Scott?"

Scott looked at her in surprise and said, "No, no not at all. How do you know my name?"

The girl laughed. "I knew you would not recognize me. I am Patti, a friend of Harriett Baird. You know, the one your friend George saved a while back. I was there when Harriett came out of the river with that monster right behind her. I nearly fainted as well."

"Oh, good grief! I am sorry I did not recognize you," responded Scott, abashed. "I take it that you are, or were, a student here?"

"Yes, I am in my fourth year. Biochemical and biomedical engineering," explained Patti.

Just then the hall erupted in a cacophony of cheering and clapping as the host moderator, Harvey Williger, stepped up to the podium. He raised his hands and the audience quieted.

"Ladies and gentlemen, I want to thank you for coming out this evening to hear our special guest speaker, Dr. James Hilitz. As you undoubtedly know, Dr. Hilitz is head of the board of directors for the Environmental and Health Protection Agency.

"Though this agency is under the auspice of the federal government, they have autonomy over their policies and procedures. This agency is highly respected in the upper chambers of government and their recommendations are seriously considered and, for the most part, mandated into practice.

"Dr. Hilitz is married, a father of two grown children, and a grandfather to three grandchildren. Dr. Hilitz and his family live in Orion City. Please welcome Dr. James Hilitz."

Again, the hall erupted into cheering and clapping as Dr. Hilitz came up to the podium. He shook hands with Harvey Williger, who took his seat behind the podium.

"Thank you, Dr. Williger, for the warm introduction. It is an honor to be here this evening. Tonight, I am going to share with you, through PowerPoint presentation who the Environmental and Health Protection Agency is and what we represent.

"First, though, let me tell you how and why the agency was created. In my younger years, some friends and I were very concerned over the loss of wildlife habitat and the significant changes happening in the natural plant world. Many species of animals and plants were becoming extinct. Further study showed that industries like manufacturing, farming, mining, and forestry were, and still are, following improper practices, such as incorrectly disposing hazardous waste, using toxic components, overusing soil, over reaping trees, and using harmful methods of getting natural resources out of the ground. Loss of habitat, soil erosion, poor air quality, potable water contamination, and a host of other problems causing health problems and economic problems, along with climate change, is putting all of us at risk. The Earth will not be able to endure much more if we do not make a sincere effort to make the necessary changes to these practices so that we all can enjoy long, healthy lives. Let us get started on the PowerPoint presentation so that you can see and fully understand what is at stake here."

Dr. Hilitz led the audience through the presentation, adding comments and explaining the different procedures that could be implemented in the times to come.

"In conclusion, everyone, we need to be more assertive and cognitive of our resources, taking care to be good stewards of this Earth. For more information on how you can become involved and help save our planet, please check out the book table setup just outside the east door. Thank you for your support."

The audience clapped and cheered. Then everyone rose from their chairs and quickly started leaving the auditorium.

Unconsciously, Scott took Patti's arm and steered her though the crowd to an open side door that led outside. A cool breeze washed away the stale indoor air.

"That was quite the talk Dr. Hilitz gave," commented Scott.

"Yes, it was," agreed Patti. "Thank you for your company, Scott."

"Oh, you're welcome. And thank you for your company. Say, how about we go to the Jumping Cow and get a drink," suggested Scott. "It will take a while for the traffic to thin out."

"That would be great. I do not drink, though," replied Patti.

"That is okay. You can have a soft drink or a coffee. They serve everything, including food," replied Scott.

At the Jumping Cow, Scott and Patti found a quiet table. The pub was busy. People were laughing and talking and enjoying themselves. Scott and Patti shared a sandwich, talking and laughing together. Soon, the Jumping Cow was emptying out of its patrons. Scott and Patti finally decided to leave, as they were both yawning. Scott offered to drive Patti home.

"Hey, listen, Patti, would you like to go out on Saturday? I finally have a day off and would love to do something fun," said Scott as he pulled up to Patti's apartment building.

"Yes, I would love to. I have not had any time for a social life between classes, projects, and work; my days are filled up," replied Patti.

"I hear you," said Scott.

Scott quickly got out of the car and went around to Patti and escorted her to the building door.

"Would you like me to pick you up or would you like to meet me at the Best Steakhouse and Grill, on Monroe Avenue?"

"I will just meet you there. What time, Scott?" answered Patti as she unlocked her building door.

"Would six thirty work for you? After dinner, we can take in a movie if you want."

"Six thirty will be just fine, so would a movie. I will see you then."

"Okay, see you then, Patti," said Scott as he turned to leave, looking over his shoulder to see Patti walking to the elevator.

The rest of the week flowed into several weeks, which flowed into months. Scott and Patti kept company, and their relationship blossomed into a deep love affair. They had so many things in common. They continued to get involved with political and social affairs. Before long, they found themselves in a quagmire of misinformation, down right lies and deceptions dressed in half-truths. They both decided to quit all of it and get out.

Things are never as they seem, thought Scott. Getting out of their situation was not as easy as getting into it. Both he and Patti were harassed, and then came the threats. Scott noticed Patti was beginning to unravel. After she wrote her final exams, she left the university, the state, and headed who knows where. She did not even tell Scott where she was going. Scott was heartbroken. He never saw her again.

Chapter 3

One day as Scott was leaving his office, a man approached him. "Mr. Scott McDonald?"

"Yes?" replied Scott, looking into the reflective sunglasses the man was wearing. He glanced over to spot another man standing off to his left.

"We need you to come with us," said the man with the sunglasses, and he flashed Scott his badge.

Scott examined the badge and asked, "What is this all about?"

"Please, sir, just come with us. All will be explained."

Though Scott had many questions, he left them unsaid during the ride. Soon, they came to a nondescript building just out of Metro Orion City. A small sign on the building said "Federal Co-op." Scott was led down some stairs to a lower level. When the doors opened, he stood speechless at what he beheld.

The entire floor was filled with computers, monitors, and all shapes and sizes of electronic devices. Uniformed people were working quietly at well-designed workstations. Channels built into the stations kept all wires and cables up off the floor. Scott noticed how clean and tidy everything was. He figured it must be a command center of some kind.

His questions were soon answered when the men led him to Agent Douglas, Commander, and Chief of Operations.

"Glad you could make it, Mr. McDonald," greeted Agent Douglas. "My name is Agent Douglas. I have been wanting to meet you for some time."

"Why?" asked Scott, now more perplexed than before.

"Oh, yes, I guess you would like an explanation. Come sit down here," said Agent Douglas as he took Scott to the back of the center. Behind a privacy screen was a sitting room with a ring of four easy chairs. Each chair had an end table beside it. In front of the chairs was an ornate coffee table, which contained a carafe of coffee, coffee mugs, and a box of donuts.

"Please be seated, Mr. McDonald. Would you like a coffee?"

"Guess so. What is this all about?" queried Scott as he took the mug of coffee handed to him.

"Yes, yes, you must have many questions and I will answer them. First, though, do you know who the Brotherhood of Theoretical Economics and Political Sciences is?"

Scott nodded.

Agent Douglas went on, "Do you understand what they stand for and who the driving force behind them is?"

Scott thought carefully before answering. He took another sip of coffee and put his cup down on the table. "I have my suspicions but no absolute proof. I avoid any contact with them and do not attend any of their rallies."

"What are your suspicions?" asked Agent Douglas.

"I believe that they are a front for those elitists who think they know better than anyone else on how this planet should be run. They want absolute control over all aspects of life, including how many people the Earth can handle. In other words, they want to deplete the population by at least one-quarter of its present number. They also want to control the world's economy. Absolute power is their game. But, as I said, I have no definite proof," answered Scott.

"What I must show you, Mr. McDonald, will help you to understand and see the proof that you are lacking," explained Agent Douglas.

A huge screen lit up on the wall opposite Scott with pictures showing all the political rallies that Scott had attended. There was no denying that he was there, for there he stood as big or bigger than life.

"Okay, so I was there. There is no law against that," said Scott, more than a little perturbed at being photographed.

"Rightly so, rightly so. Do you know this man?" Again, another picture came on screen.

"Yes, that is Jack Lang. He is the leader of the Brotherhood of Theoretical Economics and Political Sciences Chapter of Orion. I never had too much to do with him. I attended a couple of seminars. There was a woman with him . . . umm . . . oh yes, Millie Middleton. I really do not know these people personally," said Scott.

"And one last picture . . . this man?"

Scott could feel the blood leave his face. His heart beat faster, and a light film of sweat covered his skin.

"Yes, that's Vince White. He was a classmate of mine in university," said Scott.

Agent Douglas looked closely at Scott. "What is wrong? What else do you know?"

Scott turned his eyes to the agent, dreading what he had to say. Fear tightened his throat. He shook his head.

Agent Douglas stood up and said in a voice that conveyed concern, "Just relax, Mr. McDonald. I will be back in a moment."

Agent Douglas returned with a glass and a decanter of water. He poured water into the glass and handed it to Scott. Scott's throat felt parched and scratchy. He looked at the water, not trusting it.

"Do not worry, Mr. McDonald. I assure you, it is just water," said Agent Douglas as he took the glass back and took a sip, then handed it back to Scott.

Scott drank the water right down.

"Good. Now tell me about Vince White. Why were you so distressed?"

"Vince White is a bad cross between a shark and a snake. He sneaks about spying on people. Then pretending to be a help to them, he turns and tries to destroy them through intimidation and deceit. He is the worst kind of bully I have ever encountered. When he is finished with his victims, they are mere shells of who they once were, should they be lucky enough to survive. Those that do not survive are never seen nor heard of again.

"Vince White was so jealous of my best friend, George. Just because George beat him in a competition in university, he tried to kill him. George was pronounced dead but came back when an Evangelist prayed over him." Scott started rocking back and forth as the thoughts of losing George re-emerged from deep inside.

"I see," said Agent Douglas. "Relax, Mr. McDonald. Just relax; you are safe here." Agent Douglas filled Scott's glass with more water. "The reason you are here, Mr. McDonald—may I call you Scott and forget about formalities? You can just call me Douglas." Scott nodded. "The reason you are here, Scott, is that you have been attending these rallies. Do you know any other similar organizations, and what is behind them?"

"No, I do not know anything about the other organization other that what I have heard. I do know that some of these activists who support of the Brotherhood of Theoretical Economics and Political Sciences also support other similar organization. I am not fussy about their politics, nor do I care for their platform. The other rallies that I have been to are low level and not quite so extreme. Many of their ideas are based on common sense, and they really do want to make a difference. Those are the ones that I get more involved with," explained Scott.

"We are most interested in the Brotherhood of Theoretical Economics and Political Sciences. They are under the auspices of the Brotherhood of the Last Stronghold of Rights and Freedoms. Do you know who the Brotherhood of the Last Stronghold of Rights and Freedoms is or do you know anything about this organization, Scott?"

"No, I do not really know anything about this organization nor any of the players. Why? What does this have to do with me?"

"We are looking for someone who has no affiliation with us or any other governmental departments, someone who has not been deeply involved but only somewhat involved in these rallies and such. You fit the bill. You are not overly involved or connected personally with anyone in the groups we are interested in. All we would require from you is to keep your eyes and ears open. It may be, as time goes by, that you might become a little more involved. We do have people deep inside. We want peripheral information.

"Thing is, Scott, it is not always glaring information that can bring an evil organization down. Often, it is the little things. Things that most people think are irrelevant and overlooked.

"But it is the little things that fit into place to make the big picture. The danger to you would be very minimal. I believe your skills would be most beneficial to us," responded Agent Douglas. "If we do not do something more, then we will be kissing our country goodbye. These people and organizations must be stopped—at all costs.

"You are an intelligent and resourceful person. People like you and respond well to you. You would make a great contribution to our cause. Would you consider participating?"

"Agent Douglas, I would love to serve my country, I am nervous about participating, however, I will give it some consideration," replied Scott.

Chapter 4

After George's complete recovery, he finished off his fourth year of university, graduating after his fifth year with a master's degree in mechanical engineering. He continued working for the top engineering company in the country. George's reputation was growing and he was considering opening his own engineering firm in Crescent River, which was becoming a boom town. Opportunities were opening in manufacturing, forestry, farming, and mining bringing in people and money. This part of the country was coming into full economic development. Rail spurs from the main railroad were being laid down and highways were being built replacing the old road systems that had not been upgraded or taken proper care of for many decades, not since before the depression many decades ago. George had made good money and wise investments and was considered wealthy. He packed up all his things, quit his job, and headed back to Crescent River.

***

The next four years saw Scott working, attending rallies, gathering information, and passing it along. His eyes were being opened to the deceit of these rallies and he could see hidden agendas being perpetuated. Corruption, though subtle, was becoming rampant and people were being sucked into a philosophy that ran totally contrary to the rights and freedoms that the nation had enjoyed for centuries. Scott decided that now was the time to get out from under the weight he was bearing. The burden of almost losing his best friend,

George, and knowing who was behind it and being forbidden to tell him finally became too much. When Scott had heard that George was quitting his job and was going to set up his own firm back in Crescent River, he gave him a call.

"Hey, George," greeted Scott on this cell phone.

"Hey, Scott! How are you doing, man? Been awhile since I have heard from you."

"I have been so busy that time has flown by. I am doing okay. Listen, George, I was told that you were quitting your job and going to start up your own business back in Crescent River."

"Yeah, I am done here. I was going to call you and see if you were interested in coming back and working with me."

"Can tell we're best friends, actually brothers by different parents," said Scott, "That is why I'm calling. The questions are, when do we leave and how much can I invest in your company? Not on a partner basis, just would like to help you out, George."

"Good, glad to hear you are coming with me. We will talk about investment later. It will take me at least three months to finish up some contract work; get all my other ducks in a row. So, let us see, how about we leave here at the end of June?"

"Sounds great to me, George. I will have all my business finished up by then as well."

"Okay, buddy, let us get together sometime before then. We have not seen each other for a long time. Miss you."

"Right on! Will catch up with you soon. Miss you too, George."

Chapter 5

A new office tower had just been completed in Crescent River. George leased the top floor and set about having the it set up for his engineering firm. George hired a full staff and had landed a huge contract to do the mechanical work for an Oriented Strand Board Mill being built near the river. As well, he landed another contract for the mechanical work for a large mining company that was coming into the area within the next few months. Other smaller projects were coming in hot and heavy. Business was booming!

One day, as George was about to leave for the day, a young woman entered the lobby, carrying a briefcase in one hand and her phone in the other hand. She approached the receptionist and asked, "Is George Hamer in?"

"Hello, I'm George Hamer," said George, "and you are?"

"Hello, I am Harriett Baird. Do you remember me?" asked Harriett.

"Of course, I remember you!" exclaimed George. "Come back to my office. Oh, Cindy,"—he turned to the receptionist—"lock up when you leave."

"Yes, of course. Do you need anything before I leave?"

"No, that's fine, Cindy. See you tomorrow."

George led Harriett down to his office. He unlocked and opened the door and stepped aside to let her go in first.

"Lights on," said George. The lights lit up and flooded his office, giving the pale gray walls a warm glow.

Beautiful cherry wood furnishings sat on blue-gray low-pile carpeting that covered the spacious office floor. Even the large well-tinted windows were framed by cherry wood. Oyster white tub chairs were positioned neatly in front of George's desk. In front of the floor-to-ceiling bookcase sat an oyster white couch. The effect was both masculine and elegant.

"Have a seat, Harriett," he said as he motioned toward one of the chairs. George sat in his chair and took in the beauty of the girl he had rescued years before.

Harriett sat down. She took in the handsome man sitting across from her. Memories flooded her brain as she recalled that day when a dashing boy dove into the water and saved her life.

The two sat in silence for a few minutes until Harriett said, "Thank you for taking time to see me so late in the afternoon. I am here in response to your ad online for a project engineer. Also, I was not sure if you were the same George Hamer who saved my life years ago." A blush rose into her cheeks as she continued, "I-I don't mean to impose on our acquaintance for a leg up for this job."

"No . . . no," responded George reassuringly. "The thought never crossed my mind. I am glad that you came in. How have you been? What have you been doing all these years? Are you married?" George could have bitten off his tongue.

She smiled and replied, "I have been doing fine. I have been out on the West Coast going to school and working. I came back here to help my Dad since Mom passed away, and no, I am not married. And you?"

George regained his composure and replied, "I am doing well. Been busy getting my business up and running. I went the opposite direction than you. I graduated from the University of Orion and worked for a large engineering firm there for a few years. But with the opportunities opening here, I decided to return. I am not married either. Would you like to go to dinner with me this evening? There is a great steak and seafood place just around the corner. We could catch up where it is a bit more comfortable—and I am starving!"

"Yes, I would love to. But I must go home first and fix some supper for Dad. Could I meet there at, say, six thirty?" Harriett's large brown eyes met George's eyes in expectation.

"That would be fine. I will see you then."

After she left, George looked over Harriett's resume. He wrote on it and put it in his desk drawer. He smiled to himself as he thought about dinner with Harriett.

***

Harriett arrived at the restaurant promptly at six thirty to find George already seated at a quiet table for two.

George rose when he saw Harriett approaching. He pulled out the chair for her and waited for her to be seated before returning to his own chair.

"I'm sorry I'm late," said Harriett.

George looked at her in surprise. "You are not late; in fact, you are right on time. Do you want a drink, Harriett?"

"No, thank you. I will just have a coffee. I neither drink nor smoke. Have seen too many people ruin their lives."

"Yeah. I do not drink or smoke either. I never did care for alcohol, and cigarettes turn me right off. I had an incident a few years ago that more than convinced me to beware of the devastating effects of drugs and alcohol. Just about cost me my life."

Harriett looked up at George, who was staring down at his coffee cup. Harriett could see that something very significant and troubling had happened, but she did not want to pry, though she was curious.

George looked up and said, "I am sorry, Harriett. I did not mean to drift away."

George and Harriett ate in companionable silence, each enjoying their meal. They laughed as they relaxed in each other's company.

"George, I must get going. Thank you for the most pleasurable dinner. I really enjoyed myself," said Harriett as they both rose from the table.

"I really did have a good time tonight, George," Harriett said as they walked toward her vehicle. "I never got to thank you properly for saving my life. After that incident my parents started overprotecting me. I felt like I was being squashed in on all sides. Do not get me wrong; I love my parents. They are great, but they were smothering me."

"That is understandable. You are their only child and they probably cannot bear the thought of losing you. But I take it, you and your folks worked things out?"

"Oh yes! As I said, together, they were terrific. Ever since Mom passed last year, my dad has been in a funk. I have been worried, so I decided to move back here to see if I could help him. The church that I have been attending has been praying for him. Some of those ladies are widows, and there are widowers too. They have been helping me see that if we take our eyes off ourselves and put them on Jesus, then our mourning and sorrows will all pass over.

"So, I encouraged Dad to attend. So far, he has been willing to go with me. I have seen some light in his eyes. Not quite so mournful as when I first came here. Thank you again, George, for the lovely evening." Harriett smiled up at him.

"You are very welcome. It was my pleasure. I will see you soon."

Harriett nodded and opened the driver's door of her Ford Mustang and got in. She turned the key and the Mustang roared to life. She pulled out into the street and drove away. Through her rearview mirror, she could see the handsome man as he watched her car for a moment before walking back to his. She wondered what he was thinking.

When George arrived at work the next day, he was greeted by a visibly upset Scott.

"What's up, Scott?" Then nodding at Cindy, he said, "Good morning, Cindy."

"Good morning, Boss," greeted Cindy. "Here is your mail. Mr. Schwartz from the bank called. He left you a voicemail but wanted me to tell you to call him as soon as you got in."

"Thank you, Cindy. I will call him right away. Come on, Scott. Now, what has happened? What are you upset about?"

George unlocked his office door and proceeded to his desk. He laid his mail in a basket on the corner of his desk, then sat down in his chair, all the while listening to Scott as he told George what was troubling him.

"I am telling you, George, there is no way that new cutting machine is going to work. I have redesigned the whole layout, and it will not fit and it will not be efficient. We need to set up a meeting with Mr. Rigger and his son Jason," explained Scott.

"So, set up a meeting. I believe you know how to do that, don't you?"

"I cannot. Mr. Rigger passed away last night and Jason is not taking any phone calls. You know, George, this project must be completed in three months or we will lose a lot of money. And as of right now, we are already several weeks behind."

"Okay, Scott, keep working on this. I will see what I can do about Jason. But right now, I need to call Mr. Schwartz and find out what is up there."

Scott got up and walked to the door. Before he left, he paused, turned, and said, "George, we have been through a lot together. I-I just wanted to let you know how much I appreciate you and to say, thank you."

Scott walked out the door, leaving George with a bewildered look on his face. *What was that all about?* wondered George. Just then his phone rang.

Chapter 7

After Harriett's life-saving rescue, life had become burdensome for the active seventeen-year-old. Out of love and fear, Harriett's parents enveloped her in a heavy cloak of over-protectiveness. Going from a once, more-or-less, carefree teenage life to being shackled by invisible chains of oppression, Harriett longed to break free and fly like the eagles. Harriett loved her parents. She knew of their deep love for her. They provided a good home and provided for all her needs. She was hugged and kissed and encouraged in her music and education. There was always laughter and joy. However, there was no real freedom. After graduation, and a much-heated discussions with her parents, Harriett boarded the train that would take her across the country to Banta, on the West Coast, and to her dream of attending Bantine University.

"Now listen, Harriett," started her mother again in what seemed the umpteenth time, "you phone us the minute you get to your apartment. Daddy has made sure the apartment is already for you and the phone, TV, and computer are hooked up and ready to go."

"Yes, Mama, I will call you as soon as I arrive. Please, please quit worrying about me. I am nineteen and can look after myself. I will be fine. You know Jesus is looking after me."

Harriett's mother had nodded and hugged her daughter one last time.

Tears were on the verge of slipping down her dad's face as he hugged her tightly, but he quickly brushed them away. "Listen, if you need anything, anything at all, you call no matter what the time of day or night, you hear?"

"Yes, Daddy, I will." Harriett then boarded the train and found a window seat so that she could wave to her parents as the train pulled away from the platform.

Harriett had flourished in university. She tackled her courses with zeal and succeeded in receiving honors for her hard work. After five years, Harriett graduated with a master's degree in engineering and a bachelor's degree in music. She had every intention of staying in Banta, for she had secured a great job with a leading engineering firm. But life, as always, threw a curveball at her. Harriett had just opened her apartment door after returning home from work when her phone started to ring.

"Hello," said Harriett as she removed her coat.

"Harriett," came a broken voice.

"Daddy? Daddy? What is wrong? Are you there?"

Harriett pulled a tissue from her pocket and dabbed her eyes as her father told her of her mother's passing. Several hours later, her plane landed at the Crescent River airport. Harriett retrieved her carry-on bag from the overhead and disembarked the plane.

Looking for her father, she spotted him waiting by the doors. His once black hair was now white as snow. Lines, deep lines grooved down his cheeks and his forehead furrowed with more deep lines. Sad brown eyes flickered with relief and gladness when he saw his daughter coming toward him. He held out his arms and hugged his her as though she were a lifesaver.

"Oh, Daddy!" sobbed Harriett as she buried her face into his wide shoulder, the same shoulder that was always comforting and safe.

Her father patted her back and he kissed the top of her head. "Come, child. Let us go home."

Upon arriving at her childhood home, Harriett noticed that the grass needed cutting and, somehow, the house itself looked as though it was in mourning too. *How foolish*, thought Harriett, *just my imagination*. But when she walked into the house, the gloomy atmosphere was almost palpable. Though the house was tidy, emptiness filled the air.

The dog, Sparkplug, was lying dejectedly in his bed. When he saw Harriett and her dad come in, he raised his head and thumped his stubby tail, then laid his head down again. His food dish and water bowl had not been touched. Harriett went over to the pup, speaking softly to him. She picked up the black-and-white woolly poodle cross and cradled him. He licked her hand and settled into her arms.

"Daddy? Have you started the arrangements for Mom's funeral?"

"Her remains have been taken to the funeral home. I have contacted Pastor Loren. He will be coming over this afternoon to go over the arrangements. The funeral home will take care of all the paperwork. All I must do is sign the documents. Mr. Tigh will be coming this afternoon too. I am so glad you are here, honey."

Harriett fixed some lunch. She and her dad ate in silence; each one lost in their own thoughts. Soon, however, they began sharing anecdotes and stories, laughing at some of the funny things that had happened over the years.

Chapter 8

Six months after Harriett's mother's passing, Harriett had sold her condo on the West Coast, finished up some work projects, and moved back to Crescent River. Her father was ecstatic to have his daughter home.

Harriett looked her dad in the eye and saw a gleam of amusement. "What? What am I missing?"

"I have a secret! I have a secret!" exclaimed her dad with a wide grin.

"What? What? What is your secret?"

"Cannot tell you. At least not until tomorrow night. Oh, which reminds me, you and I are going to a dinner party tomorrow night at the Magpie Inn. It is a formal affair hosted by Riggs and Mortimer Evangelical ministries. It is a fundraising event, with the proceeds going to mission work in the Congo, Africa. This kicks off the week-long convention with speakers coming from all over, including speakers from abroad.

"Everyone is welcome to come and join the services that will be held daily for four days. But the dinner party tomorrow night is by invitation, and I have secured a ticket for you. So, I will meet you at the inn at five o'clock." With that, he put on his jacket, picked up his keys off the table, kissed his daughter, and left her apartment and went home, leaving Harriett both baffled and extremely curious as to what this great secret could be about.

The next evening, Harriett put on a mid-calf peach chiffon gown, which accentuated her hour-glass figure before billowing down from a dropped waistline. Picking up her matching handbag and a white fur wrap, Harriett left her apartment, locked the door, and went down the street to a waiting cab.

Her father met her outside the Magpie Inn. "Oh! You look beautiful, honey! And I see you are on time. Would not have expected anything less." He laughed as he took hold of Harriett's arm and led her inside to the banquet hall.

Harriett looked up at her dad and marveled at how well he looked. He stood straight and tall. His curly white hair was cut short, accentuating his high forehead.

His dark complexion was still impaled with lines and wrinkles, but what she noticed the most was the sparkle in his deep brown eyes and a grin that was radiant. As Harriett took her place beside her dad, she noticed a well-groomed woman sitting on the chair next to him. Harriett nodded to the woman and turned her attention to a gentleman sitting next to her, who greeted her.

"Hello, Harriett," said the gentleman.

"Well, hello, Mr. Grainger! How are you?"

"I am just fine, Harriett. Please, just call me Ben. I have not seen you for years. Are you keeping well?"

"Oh yes. I moved back here some months ago. Now, I must get serious and look for a job."

"I am glad to hear you are doing well. There are plenty of job opportunities out here. I wish you well, Harriett."

"Thank you, Ben. It is good to see you again."

Just then Harriett's dad touched her arm. She turned her attention to him.

"Harriett, I would like to introduce you to Agatha Carlyle. Agatha, this is my daughter, Harriett."

"Hello, Agatha. Nice to meet you," said Harriett.

"Hello, Harriett. It is a pleasure to meet you. Your father has told me so much about you."

Harriett looked questioningly at her dad. He smiled back and said, "This is the secret I was talking about. Agatha and I have been seeing each other for the past few months. So, I thought it was time for you two to meet."

"I . . ." started Harriett. She then gave a strangled chuckle and said again, "This is nice. Congratulations."

"Didn't your dad tell you, Harriett?" asked Agatha as she looked accusingly at her father.

Harriett shook her head no.

"Really, Ralph! Why didn't you say something to her? You should have said something to her instead of springing it on her like this," scolded Agatha in a gentle voice.

"Harriett, I am so sorry. I think sometimes men just do not get things, let alone have any understanding of things."

All kinds of emotions swept through Harriett, but she kept her composure throughout the rest of the evening. Soon, everyone was eating their meals, and finally, the guest speaker was introduced. As the evening progressed, Harriett, who loved to hear testimonies and hear about other people's healing and salvation, was ready to go home. She excused herself and said good night to her dad and Agatha.

At home, Harriett changed out of her good clothes, jumped into the shower, and washed and shampooed her hair. After drying her hair, she put on her nightwear and was ready for bed. Harriett laid down on her bed as tears flowed down her cheeks. *How could he do this with Mama being gone less than a year? Didn't he love her? Why does he want to get involved with another woman?*

These thoughts and emotions rolled around her brain until she could not stand it any longer. She got up and went into her living room. She saw her Bible sitting open at Genesis, where Chapter 2, Verse 18 was underlined. She read the verse out loud: *"And the Lord God said, 'It is not good that man should live alone; I will make a helper comparable to him.'"*

Tears again overflowed her eyes and fell onto her Bible. She took some tissue and dabbed them. She thumbed through her Bible until she came to the Book of Joshua. Harriett and her Bible study group were studying Joshua. She looked at Chapter 1 and received revelation of what God told Joshua. *"After the death of Moses, the servant of the Lord, it came to pass that the Lord spoke to Joshua the son of Nun,*

Moses's assistant saying: Moses, My servant, is dead. Now therefore, arise, go over this Jordan, you and all these people, to the land which I am giving them—the children of Israel." Harriett pondered this passage. Then she recalled something her mama had once said when her sister passed away: "*Life stops for no one. When one passes from this life, they pass into a glorious life with Christ, if they died in faith. Those who are left must arise and carry on until their time comes.*"

"Mourning for the dead leads to idolatry if carried on. One must be flexible to change and move forward with their lives. Though our loved ones leave us, our Heavenly Father will never leave us nor forsake us. So, we must be strong and of good courage and face our futures with faith and confidence."

Harriett sat in her chair with her eyes shut, and it was as though her mother was in the room talking to her. She could smell her mother's favorite perfume and could feel her hand touch her face oh so softly. Harriett opened her eyes half-expectantly to see her mother's face, but no one was there. Peace of such magnitude filled her that she could hardly move. Soon, she was fast asleep.

Over the next several weeks, Harriett got to know Agatha better and realized that Agatha was good for her dad; he flourished under Agatha's love and care. When the announcement had come that Agatha and Ralph were to marry in one month's time, Harriett was thrilled.

Chapter 9

George had settled in and called Mr. Schwartz at the bank. "Hello, Henry. You called. Sounded urgent. What is up?" inquired George.

"Well, George . . . I know there must be some terrible mistake, but your company account has been totally drained. We have checked out our end to see if there has been some kind of computer glitch, but everything checks out fine. I want you to get your accounting department to do a thorough financial report immediately and come over to see me tomorrow morning at nine o'clock. We cannot cover any of your expenses that would be coming through today. We need documents filed for insurance purposes so that the money can be replaced as soon as possible. I am very sorry, George. I just do not understand this."

George held his phone tightly in his hand as a deep sense of panic, anger, and confusion enveloped him.

"That cannot be right! I will get on it right away!" George hung up his phone and dashed out of his office and hurried to the accounting department. When he arrived, he found the whole department in an uproar. People were talking and shouting. IT people were rushing in and out, checking computers, gathering information. As soon as George walked in, dead silence veiled the room. Everyone stopped what they were doing and stared at George.

"Where's Gloria?" asked George in a false calm voice.

"I'm right here, Boss."

George and Gloria went into her office, closing the door behind them. He looked expectantly at her. Just then there was a knock at the door. When the door opened, Mitchell, head of the information technology department, stepped in.

"Hey, Boss. Gloria. We have been breached. Happened about two o'clock this morning. My guys are tracing where it came from. Do not know if we'll ever find out. These intruders are extremely clever and knowledgeable. They seldom leave a trail. But if they did, we will find it. They bounce off different satellites and towers all around the world. Becomes a nightmare web of tangled string," explained Mitchell as he sat down on a chair next to George.

"I have so many questions. But first things first. Gloria, I need forensic account reports ready for me to take to the bank before nine o'clock tomorrow morning. Mitchell, is there any way we can stop this leak right now?"

Mitchell replied, "We will have to make major changes to the operating system. Our firewall should not have been able to be breached. . . ." Mitchell became uneasy with what he was about to say.

"Spit it out Mitchell," said George. "What is it?"

"Well, I am not sure. I'm checking it out, but I would hate to say that this might have been an inside job. You see," said Mitchell as he leaned forward in his chair, "there was no warning. We have the best anti-breaching system on the market. Our firewalls are state-of-the-art. There is just no way that anyone can get into our system from the outside without alarms going off. I designed and constructed this system myself. The only way anyone could get into the system would be to go through either the main frame—which would be impossible—or to go through your computer, Boss. That would be difficult as well. There are so many protocols and tight security controls to get through. It would take hours to figure out. The only other way is if someone left their security code in sight. People do it all the time. Then, though it would still be tough, they could get in through a lower-level computer station. It must have been an inside job, or through carelessness." Mitchell leaned back in perplexity and pondered the situation in his head. "Boss, I need to get back and continue with what I was doing," said Mitchell as he rose to his feet.

"Can we still print off these reports I need?" asked George.

"Yes, they should not take too long to print off. I have shut down all external access. But we can still run through the internal system. We must let the authorities know right away. I have called the police," said Mitchell. "Do not worry, Boss, we will get to the bottom of this. I will catch you later."

Chapter 10

Less than an hour later, the cyber-crime team came in and commandeered the whole IT and the accounting departments. Everyone was rushing to put reports in order. All hard copies were stacked in file folders and placed in order of importance, labeled, and stacked on wheeled tray tables and given over to the appropriate cyber team member. Soon, agents from the Internal Revenue Services showed up as well as regular patrolmen to secure the premises.

George was doing his best to keep calm when both Gloria and Mitchell came through his door.

"This is bad, George," said a harried and worried Gloria. "It isn't just funds missing; I managed to print out some of the account receivables, which have been given to the agents, but some of them have been tampered with. I told the agent there, but she did not seem concerned. I do not know, George, this could make it seem as if there is fraud going on here."

Mitchell's voice was tense when he added, "Not just that, but a Trojan horse was downloaded. All our files are now corrupted. Even the backup of the backups are corrupted! But there is one shining bit of news. Now, George, please do not get upset. I should have told you what I was doing, but I have another computer set up offsite in a secure location. I designed it myself. All the information that is now corrupted is secure. I will redirect it back into this system once we do a thorough systems clean up. But there could be some backlash. It is highly illegal and suspicious for me to have done that.

"It is funny, not ha-ha funny, but strange funny. I only did all this three nights ago. I had no idea that this would happen. But I had heard on the news that in another country this same thing happened. It bothered me to think that something like this could happen with all the security and firewalls that have improved so much over the past years. But I thought, what if I just back up everything one more time in a different place? I knew I could do it without leaving any footprints. So, as an experiment, that is what I did. I was going to tell you, but we have been so busy, I did not get a chance to."

George squinted his eyes shut and clenched his teeth. "I thought that our system was good enough for things like this. I am not going to worry about the illegality of what you did, Mitchell. We will deal with that later. I just wished that you had told me sooner." George paused and drew in a deep breath. "Gloria, would you get all the team leaders together in the boardroom in fifteen minutes? I will meet everyone there."

Just then, there was a knock on the door and the lead cyber officer entered. He was a short muscular man with gray buzzed-cut hair. His icy-blue eyes darted everywhere before landing on George.

"Do you need something, Officer?" asked George, watching the officer carefully. George nodded his head in dismissal to Gloria and Mitchell, who hurried out of the office to avoid the fireworks that seemed about ready to go off.

"I am Chief Commander Schultz of the Special Ops Cyber Team. Looks as though you are in a whole heap of trouble, son. You will have to shut down your business until this is all cleared up," said Schultz in a rough gravelly voice. "All your personal and business accounts are frozen as well as all your employees' personal accounts. We believe that this was an inside job."

George's stress level leaped, but he kept his calm and said, "I do not believe for a moment that this is an inside job. I will be speaking to my attorneys."

"Good plan. Things do not bode well for those who cheat, steal, or kill," said Schultz as his heated stare bore a hole into George. George returned the stare without a blink. A moment passed before Schultz dropped his eyes, turned on his heel, and left George's office.

George drew in a full breath again and released it slowly, then left his office and headed for the boardroom. The boardroom was eerily quiet: no one was on their phone, no one was speaking. Their phones had been confiscated as well as all laptop computers and tablets. The atmosphere was tight with tension;

"Okay, everyone, we have a problem," said George as he came through the door and went to his chair and sat down. "I've been instructed to shut down the office until this investigation is over. I do not know how long it will take," explained George as everyone groaned.

"I was also told that everyone's bank account is now frozen." George watched as everyone's faces turned to horror. The thought of not being able to access their account and having their cell phone taken away led them from horror to anger. George, himself, was starting to get more and more angry.

"But that is not all," said George. "They think that this was an inside job. I personally do not think so. There must be another explanation. Listen! This may look bad right now, but I believe all this will be settled before too long. I am going to see my attorney. If some of you need a few dollars, please see Gloria. She will give you what you need. But please just ask for the smallest amount that you will need in the short term. If things go longer than a week or so, I will see to it that you will have what you need. Team leaders, please pass this along to your team members."

Miss Hampton, a small, thin elderly woman past retirement age who was the head of human resources, raised her hand. George nodded at her to speak.

"I had to hand over a list of all our employees and their personal information. They wanted to know if anyone was away sick or on holidays. The only one away is Scott. I do not know if he is sick or what. He has not called in."

George recalled his last meeting with Scott and the odd comment he had made. He made a note on his memo pad.

"Listen, everyone, you may as well go home. There is nothing to do here. Send the rest of your teams home too. They will be checking briefcases as you leave, so you may want to consider leaving them here," said George as he got up from his chair.

Chapter 11

George returned to his office and telephoned Henry. "Does not look like I will be able to get those reports you asked for. The feds are here and have seized all my accounts and computers."

"They got there faster than I thought they would. That is okay, George. We do not need to worry about those reports now. At the behest of your lawyer, I am expediting your insurance claim for the monies that were stolen. As soon as your accounts are open again, I will make sure that the money is deposited. But be very careful, George, and watch your back. No telling where all this will lead."

George acknowledged what the banker had said as he sat in silence contemplating this situation and what his next move would be. How could this have happened? Where was Scott? An inside job? Impossible! He trusted every one of his employees. He vetted them out very carefully before hiring them.

"Dear Lord Jesus, help me, please. Help me find out who is behind this and save my company and my reputation. Thank you, Jesus," prayed George. Just then, there was a knock on his door and Mitchell entered. George looked up in time to see a pleased look float across Mitchell's face.

"Mitchell, what are you looking so pleased about?" asked George incredulously.

"Well," started Mitchell, "before the feds arrived, I downloaded all our surveillance tapes and stored them on the Cloud. I know that the feds think this is an inside job, but I do not believe that for an instant. No one in their right mind would do this sort of thing from their computer here. So, keeping that in mind, I thought of different scenarios, and then I thought, what if someone from outside could do something like this?" Mitchell paused. "So, I thought let's cover that base."

"But, Mitchell, we can't use any of our computers," said George.

"Aw, Boss, have a little faith in me. I downloaded it to my wife's cell phone; then I covered that track. Will not hold forever, but it should give us a little time. So, let us meet at your place, and I can download from the Cloud to your computer. You do have a home computer, don't you?"

George gave Mitchell a quizzical look and shook his head no. "I always use my laptop, which you realize has been confiscated. But I have an idea," said George.

***

George and Mitchell found themselves sitting in Harriett's living room, watching the surveillance tapes. Harriett had made coffee and brought it and a plate of cookies into the living room and set everything on the coffee table.

After watching several hours of tapes, George sighed, and said, "I cannot see anything that is useful. Do you see anything, Mitchell?"

"No, I guess this was a waste of time. I was really hoping for something."

"Oh well, it was worth a try. Thanks, Mitchell."

"I must get home. Let me know of any further developments or if there is anything I can do to help," said Mitchell as he walked to the door.

Harriett closed the door behind Mitchell and walked back to the living room, gathered up the dishes from the coffee table, took them into the kitchen, rinsed them, and placed them in the dishwasher. She turned around to find George standing there, watching her. He strode over to her and gathered her into his arms and kissed her. Harriett's hands were on his shoulders as if to push him away, but instead, her arms, as if by themselves, curled around his neck and she kissed him back.

"I am . . . I am sorry, Harriett. I . . . should not have done that," said George as he released her and pulled back. "But I couldn't help myself; you are so beautiful."

"Do not apologize, George. I kissed you back, and it was such a nice kiss." Harriett smiled up at him.

"Then you're not mad or upset with me?"

"Of course not," said Harriett with a mischievous grin. "I have dreamed of you kissing me since I was seventeen! And I was right, no one could kiss better than you! You just proved it!"

"I've dreamed of kissing you since I was eighteen!"

Both George and Harriett laughed over that. They retreated into the living room and sat down on the couch.

"George, save those tapes to my hard drive. You can swing by at any time to watch them. You and Mitchell may have missed something. It seems to me that when one is stressed, one seems to miss things, so come over anytime."

"Thanks, Harriett, I'll do that right now," said George, and he saved the tapes to her hard drive. "Now, I must get going. I will see you tomorrow." He dropped a kiss on her forehead and walked out the door.

Down on the pavement, George looked upward and spotted Harriett, standing in her living room window. She raised her hand in a sweeping wave and George could hear her faint laughter in between honking car horns. He threw her a kiss, which she caught and buried her face in her hands. George laughed and waved once more before climbing into his car.

Chapter 12

George mulled over what he had seen on the videos but could not recall anything out of the ordinary. As he pulled into his driveway, he noticed the back of a black van parked on the other side of his garage. He might have missed it except that the taillights flashed on. Carefully, keeping his eyes on the taillights, George slowly opened his door. He was about to step out when a voice said quietly but deadly, "Stay where you are. You want to live, get back in and close the door."

George turned his head toward the voice only to see a masked man with a pistol aimed at him. George pulled his leg back into the car and closed the door. The man in the mask ran over to the van, dived into the now opened side door, and pulled the door closed as the van plunged backwards on the driveway and sped out of the yard kicking up loose gravel.

George, whose heart was thumping like a kettle drum, scrambled out of his car, raced through the open front door, and came to a sudden stop. He could not believe what his eyes were seeing! His entire living room had been totally ransacked.

There was not one piece of furniture left standing. Everything was torn apart, broken to pieces; even the walls had great gaping holes in them. The big picture window had been shattered. George wandered through his once beautiful home, finding not one untouched thing. George found one kitchen chair that was intact. Setting it on its legs, he gingerly sat down, making sure it would support his weight. Then he called the police.

When the police arrived, George was still sitting on the kitchen chair, with his cell phone up to his ear. He had been trying to get ahold of Scott, but so far, he had been unsuccessful.

"Mr. Hamer, this place is a disaster. You cannot stay here. We are securing this place. Do you not have alarmed security here?" asked Sergeant O'Malley of Crescent River City Police.

"Um . . . yes, I do. In fact, I have cameras installed. Let us go down in the basement. That is where my system is set up. I cannot believe that the alarms did not go off," said George, coming out of his shock. He and Sergeant O'Malley went down to the basement. Anger started to rise in George's chest.

"This is odd," said the sergeant. "Nothing has been touched down here. I expected this to be vandalized as well. What time did you say got home, Mr. Hamer?"

George shot him a sharp look and retorted, "I arrived home about five minutes before I called you. Do not think for two minutes that I did this. That is insane!"

"Well, I had to ask. Maybe they did not have time before you showed up. What do you think they wanted?"

"I do not know, but something fishy is going on. My business was breached this morning and now this." George turned on the computer monitors. He groaned. "Oh no—no images."

"I think," said the sergeant, "that these fellas knew about your system."

"You are undoubtedly right, Sergeant, but I have a backup. I installed security around my place as a precaution since our little city is quickly growing and with it comes some unsavory people," said George as he bolted up the stairs and went outside.

He had set up a set of trail cameras around the property and began gathering every tiny camera from all the inconspicuous places he had set them. Together, George and Sergeant O'Malley brought them to the police van that is used for surveillance. The van was high enough for George to stand up in and wide enough to for two work tables and two chairs, along with all the surveillance equipment. George had never seen one of these vans in person, just in movies, and he was quite impressed.

After reviewing the photos, which took a couple of hours, there was not much to see—mostly birds, cats, leaves, and such—until they came to near the last pictures. There stood a man George recognized—or at least he thought he did. The man looked like the one of the night janitors he had seen on Harriett's computer earlier in the day.

Sergeant O'Malley picked up George's tenseness. "You recognize him?"

"Well, yes, at least, I think so. I am not sure. I think I saw him last night. He looks like one of the custodians that clean the offices, but I am not a hundred percent sure," replied George.

Just then the back door of the van opened and a young officer stood there and said, "Mr. Hamer, we need you to come with us down to headquarters and give us a statement."

"Okay. Can I take my car and meet you there?"

The young cop looked past George to Sergeant O'Malley, who nodded. "Yes, that would be fine, sir. Follow me."

After a few hours at police headquarters, George returned home to find the forensic team still going through his place. Sergeant O'Malley met him at the door.

"Sorry, Mr. Hamer, but you can't come in," said O'Malley.

"I just wanted to pick up some personal things and then leave."

"I am sorry, sir. You cannot come back until we are done," said the sergeant, taking a slightly more aggressive stance.

George left and went to a local department store. He picked up some personal items and several changes of clothes, then checked into a nearby hotel. He phoned Scott again, but there was still no answer. Giving up, George jumped into a hot shower, then climbed into bed and fell into a deep sleep.

***

The next morning, George called his insurance company and set up an appointment to start a claim on his business and his house. George arrived at his insurance company in time to meet with his insurance agent, Tiffany.

"Good morning, George. Have a seat. You sure have had a bad time of it. What a run of bad luck!" said Tiffany as she brought up George's information on the computer.

He smiled and then chuckled, which in turn became laughter. Tiffany looked at him quizzically.

"Listen, my nerves have been stretched, and I am trying to see the humor in this. If that old devil thinks he can get the best of me, well, I have news for him. I praise the Lord Most High for His grace and mercy. There is not anything that has happened that cannot be fixed. So, what do you need from me?"

"I will need confirmation of your financial losses, both monies in the bank, your accounts payable and receivable, as well as other assesses that have been affected. So, what I need is a full financial report," replied Tiffany. "Here is a list of everything I need to put a claim in for the business." Tiffany turned to take the printed copy from the printer and handed it to George.

"Now," she continued, "let's get started on your home." Tiffany brought up George's residential account and started perusing the details of his insurance policy.

"You are insured for five and a half million. Now, what I need from you is a detailed copy of the damages, replacement costs, and all warranties on any electronics, household appliances, etcetera. I will also require three estimates for all repair work required to bring your residence up to the condition it was in prior to this incident. We will be sending out an adjuster when the police have completed their preliminary investigation."

George signed some documents to get the ball rolling. As George was leaving the insurance office, he spied Harriett walking up the street toward him.

"Oh, hi, George. I heard about what happened at your place last night. I am very sorry to hear about that. Why didn't you call me?"

"I was so tired and frustrated that I just went and booked a hotel room. Where are you off to?"

"I am just heading up to the bank. Have some business to take care of."

"I have time for a coffee and something to eat before I complete all the stuff I must do. Would you care to join me? I will buy you breakfast."

"Sure, George, I'd love to, but I need to go to the bank first."

"Okay, I was thinking of Tiny Tim's. Is that okay with you?"

"Oh yes, I'll meet you there in about ten minutes."

Harriett hurried on her way. George crossed the street and entered Tiny Tim's. He took a table by the window and sat down.

A waitress with a coffee pot in one hand and a menu in the other hand approached George's table. "Our special today is eggs Benedict with hash browns, toast, and bacon, ham, or sausage," said the waitress as she poured a steaming cup of coffee.

"Thank you," said George. "I'm waiting for someone to join me in a few minutes."

Harriett entered the diner and found George being poured a second cup of coffee. She went over to his table and sat down.

"Glad that little job is done," said Harriett.

"Is everything okay?" asked George as he turned her coffee cup over.

"Oh yes. I just signed some final papers for full ownership of my condo. I paid off the last little bit of the mortgage, and now I am a true homeowner. I am so happy about that. I did not have a big mortgage. I had some property out West, which I had sold and the money had come through, so I paid off my condo. It feels good," explained Harriett.

"Oh, Harriett, I am happy for you. I know what you mean. I own my place out right too, but what a disaster it is. I just finished up at the insurance company, and all the hoops I will have to jump through to get my money is ridiculous. But that is the way it is. Anyways, let us not dwell on my troubles. Let us just enjoy breakfast."

After George and Harriett finished their meal, they relaxed with another cup of coffee.

"So, George, what is going on? This is just too bazaar to say the least."

"I know," said George. "None of it makes any sense to me. I have been trying to come up with a plausible explanation and there just isn't any."

Frustration mixed with anger started to surge through George. He turned his head to look out the window and calm himself down. Then he saw the man he had seen in the video. It was the same man that George and Mitchell had watched on Harriett's television. As George watched, the man entered a bar across the street.

"Interesting," said George. "That guy we saw in the video just walked into that bar. Odd that he would be going into a bar at this time of morning. It is closed, but I saw someone open the door for him."

George paid the waitress for the breakfast. Outside the diner, George continued to keep an eye on the bar.

"Thanks for the breakfast, George. Do you think this guy had anything to do with what has been happening?"

"Not sure, but he has not worked as a custodian at my place for very long. I contract out the janitorial services. I am going to go talk to the company's administration and see what I can find out. It may not mean anything, but that bar is owned by a big crime family out of Orion City. No one would go there at this time of day unless they had business there."

"Oh, scary stuff. That gives me goosebumps," said Harriett as her shoulders shivered. "Well, I must get going. Thanks again for the breakfast."

"You are very welcome. Say, would you like to out for dinner tonight?"

"That would be nice, but how about coming to my place for dinner? I have a couple of steaks, one with your name on it. We could barbecue them."

"Sounds great, Harriett. What time?"

"How about six thirty?"

Chapter 13

George went back to his hotel suite and made a quick call to Mitchell. They agreed to meet in the afternoon at George's hotel restaurant. He then set up a meeting with his janitorial service for the following morning.

He left the hotel and went to his office to see how things were progressing there. When he arrived, he found the federal forensic accounting team going through all his books. The IT people were still going through George's computer systems.

"Mr. Hamer, you cannot be here. You must leave," said the officer in charge.

"Listen, this is my business and I need to know how much longer you guys will be," responded George tersely. "I need to get my staff back as soon as possible. I have very time sensitive contracts to fulfill."

"Well, we should be completed by the end of the week, depending on what we find," said the officer as he escorted George to the doors. George stood on the sidewalk seething. He headed to his lawyer's office.

"George! I have been waiting for you! I knew you would just show up without an appointment, so I cleared my calendar for you. Come in! Come in!" exclaimed Mr. Lewis as he led George from the reception area to his office.

Mr. James Lewis was a small rotund man who sort of waddled as he walked. His balding head shone under the lights in the hallway.

George found himself seated in a nice chair facing his lawyer. He looked into the shrewd brown eyes of his attorney, knowing that this man was extremely clever but extremely upright in judgment and character.

"Thanks, James. I should have made an appointment. Thank you for taking the time to see me," said George.

"Pish posh, that is what I am here for. Now tell me, George, what is happening?"

George told James everything, including his suspicions about the night janitor.

"George, you should have called me yesterday. This is not good—not good at all. However, I will set up my own investigation, and I will pay a visit to the feds myself. See if we cannot hurry this along. Did you bring your insurance documents? I will take care of that as well. We need to get you back into your home as soon as possible."

"Yeah, I was going to call you last night when I got home . . . but, well you know. I will get the documents tomorrow from the insurance company and bring them over to you."

"Listen, George, these policemen cannot and should not be questioning you without your lawyer present. So, call me the minute they want to question you or even if they just want to talk to you. Just tell them to speak to your lawyer, okay?"

"Yes, James, I will do that," replied George.

Nothing missed James Lewis's notice; he was as shrewd as a snake, and in the courtroom, he was fierce and contentious. Very few lawyers or even prosecutors wanted to go up against him.

"Okay, George, I will talk to you again soon. Do not worry about anything. We will get this taken care of soon," reassured James as George left his office.

While walking to his car, George began to feel more confident that everything would work out. He started his car, sat for a moment, and tried to call Scott again. Still no answer. George decided to drive over to Scott's house. Scott never went anywhere without letting George know where he would be. Since George's incident with the drug-laced drink he had ingested several years ago, Scott hovered around George like an old mother hen. This often led to tensions between the two men. George knew that Scott meant well, but good grief, George was a grown man and could take care of himself quite easily. Now it was George's turn to worry about Scott—and George did not like that one bit. Worry, to George, was paramount to being a slave to alcohol or drugs. Not worth it . . . not worth it at all. But this thought did not alleviate George's concern for his friend.

Arriving at Scott's house, George noticed Scott's Toyota truck in the driveway. He got out of his car and walked around the vehicle. Nothing unusual there, observed George. He then walked up to the front door and rang the doorbell. He tried the door, but it was locked. George walked around to the back, glancing through the windows he passed.

George peered through the kitchen window and saw what he thought was a person or something rumpled on the floor, just inside the dining room. He looked through the sliding glass doors and into the dining room. There laying on the floor was his best friend, Scott. George quickly pulled on the sliding glass door and it opened. He hurried in, knelt beside Scott, and felt for a pulse. It was there but weak. Quickly, George pulled out his cell phone and called for an ambulance. George carefully examined Scott without moving him too much. Scott's face was battered and bruised, but it was his hands that disturbed George. Every finger on Scott's hands seemed to be broken and looked like they were put through a meat grinder. His wrists were roped, burned, and bent in an awkward position.

Tenderly, George spoke to Scott. "Hey, buddy, what happened to you? I was so worried. You will be all right. Hang in there. Help is on the way."

Tears threatened to overflow George's eyes. He brushed them away and prayed. "Father in Heaven, please take care of my friend. He is Your child. I do not know what I'd do without him. Keep him in Your loving hands and heal him. In Jesus Name, Amen."

Just then the ambulance arrived. George hurried to unlock the door and let them in. Following them were the police. A flurry of activity ensued as the EMTs worked on Scott. The police were looking through the house.

An officer approached George with an unopened envelope in her hand.

"Mr. Hamer, do you know what this letter means? It is addressed to you. We found it on Scott's night stand beside his bed. Here, put these gloves on before you handle the envelope."

George took the unopened envelope in his gloved hand, opened it, and read the letter:

Dear George,

If you are reading this, then they have killed me. I tried to stop them. They would not listen. I told them that you were not the one they should come after. I am sorry, George. I did everything I could do to protect you. Be very careful. These guys are dangerous.

The letter was not signed, in fact, it did not even look finished. Puzzled, George handed the letter back to the officer.

"I have no idea what this is all about," said George

The EMTs had put Scott, who was hooked up to a heart monitor and an intravenous, onto a gurney and wheeled him out to the waiting ambulance. They loaded him into the back of the ambulance and sped off to the hospital.

Chapter 14

George was instructed to report to police headquarters to make an official statement. He was anxious to go to the hospital, but the police were insistent that he go to headquarters first.

"Have a seat, Mr. Hamer," said the police officer as he led George into an interview room. George followed him in and sat on a stark, straight-backed chair.

"Relax, Mr. Hamer. You are not here for questioning. Just here to fill out some forms and write out your statement," said the officer. He handed George some documents and a pen.

"Take your time and describe exactly what you did and saw. Also give the reason you went over to see Mr. McDonald. I will be back in about thirty minutes." The officer rose and left George alone to his task.

Thirty minutes later, the officer returned just as George was signing the completed documents. The officer scanned the forms and said, "Okay, Mr. Hamer, you can go now. We will be in touch should we have any further questions for you. By the way, we would like to take your fingerprints for exclusion purposes, with your permission, of course."

George agreed, and when that was done, he took his leave and went straight to the hospital. On his way, he called Harriett and asked her to meet him there. They arrived at the hospital at the same time, and together, they walked up to the emergency door entrance. George filled Harriett in as they proceeded to the nurses' station.

"Mr. McDonald is being examined by the doctor. I have left a message for the doctor that you are here. He will come see you when he is done," said a nurse. "Please go and have a seat in the waiting room just around the corner."

George and Harriett found an unoccupied couch and sat down to wait. The waiting room was busy with people coming and going. Seeing many people with different ailments and injuries waiting to be seen did not alleviate any tension that George was experiencing, but he was sure glad that Harriett was with him.

"George, can you think of anything that might make sense of all of this?" Harriett put her hand over his large hand and gave it a pat.

George entwined his fingers into hers. "No, I can't. I really can't! I have been mulling it over and over. Nothing makes sense—none of it," said George. With her hand in his, George felt a little of the stress leave his body. He turned his head and smiled at her.

"Thank you for coming. I did not want to face this alone. You are the only one I could think of to call. Boy, you sure look beautiful."

Harriett smiled back at him. "Thank you for thinking of me. I am glad you called."

Each sat in silence. George thought about Scott and all the things that had happened. He also thought about Harriett. As if reading each other's mind, they looked at each other and smiled. Had she been thinking about the same things too?

"Mr. Hamer? You can come in now. Mr. McDonald is in cubical eight," said the unit nurse. She buzzed the door open for them, and they entered in and proceeded to cubicle eight just as the doctor was leaving.

"Mr. Hamer, your friend has some very extensive trauma to his torso. His fingers are badly broken. He was likely beaten with a baseball bat or something like it. He has some severe burns to his arms and torso as well—cigarette burns by the looks of it. His face has been punched, with severe contusions to his mouth and eyes. A couple of teeth have been broken. He has some broken ribs and the X-rays also show a punctured lung. He will be heading up to surgery, which will take at least a couple of hours. He will be in recovery, then placed into the Intensive Care Unit. So, if you want, you can wait upstairs until the surgery is over. Take the elevator to the fourth floor and follow the blue line on the floor." With that, the doctor excused himself and went about his business.

George and Harriett went up to the fourth floor, found the surgical waiting room, and seated themselves on a couch to wait. George got up and went over to the nurses' station, letting the nurse know that they were waiting for Scott.

"That is fine, Mr. Hamer. We will let you know when the surgery is over and he's in recovery." The nurse smiled at him and turned back to her paperwork.

Returning to the couch, George chatted with Harriett and then each read magazines that were sitting on a table. To George, there was nothing worse than having to wait. Finally, George took out his phone and opened a notebook app and started making notes. He read over what he had written, trying to see if there was any pattern to what had happened, but nothing emerged.

A few hours later, the surgeon came out and spoke to George and Harriett.

"Mr. McDonald pulled through the surgery, but there is a lot of internal and external bruising. We have repaired his jaw. It is wired shut and will be that way for a few weeks. He is in recovery right now. We will be moving him to ICU in a few hours. You may as well go home. You will not be able to see him until at least tomorrow. An orthopedic surgeon has seen him too. Mr. McDonald will need surgery to his hands. That surgery will take at least three to six hours, so we are going to leave it until later in the week. He has a lot of recovery time coming up. He is a very lucky young man. Most people with this extent of injuries would not have even pulled through. He is a very lucky young man," explained the doctor.

Chapter 15

George and Harriett left the hospital and arrived at her apartment in time to see the same man who was in the video coming out of the apartment building. Quickly, George parked his vehicle, got out, and followed the man down the street. The man ducked into a nearby alley. When George reached the alley, the man had disappeared. George went down the alley a little way but could see no sign of the man. He turned around and headed back to Harriett's. When he arrived, Harriett was waiting just inside the door.

"I lost him."

"Well, I am rather glad you did because I was worried that something could have happened to you. By the sounds of it, that guy is dangerous," responded Harriett as she opened her apartment door. She headed for the kitchen to brew some coffee and put out some home-baked muffins on a plate. When she returned to the living room, she found George sitting on the couch with his head resting on the top of the couch's back.

"Are you okay?" asked Harriett as she came to sit beside him.

"Yes. I was just thinking, why would that guy be here?"

"Hmmm . . . I do not know," said Harriett as she got back up and went to get the coffee and muffins. She came back and handed a cup of coffee to George and placed the plate of muffins on the coffee table in front of him.

"Thanks," said George, taking a sip of the strong black coffee.

"I wonder what that guy was doing coming out of this building," said George again. "It's really got me curious."

George looked around Harriett's living room and could see nothing out of order. "Does not seem as though there is anything out of place. Is there, Harriett?"

"No," answered Harriett. "Hang on a second." She got up and went over to her entertainment center. She was looking at a decorative porcelain angle ornament that was slightly askew.

"Someone has been in here," she said. "Look. This porcelain angle does not belong here. This one belongs beside the television, and that willow one over there belongs here," explained Harriett as she walked over to the TV and picked up the ornament. When she did, a small speaker fell out the bottom of it. Harriett walked over to the other ornament and looked at it carefully. There in the very center of it was a tiny camera. She replaced both ornaments and stood in front of the camera with her back turned, and put her finger to her lips. George, picking up on her signal, rose from the couch with his coffee cup in his hand and walked into the kitchen.

"Say, Harriett, instead of steaks we were going to have today, how about we go out for a bite to eat?"

"Sounds good to me, I am starving. Let me get my jacket," replied Harriett as she took her coffee cup and the plate of muffins into the kitchen. She returned to the living room, picked up her jacket and keys, and left the apartment, locking the door behind them.

"Listen, Harriett, this is getting dangerous. Would you consider going to your dad's place for a few days?"

"I do not know. It bugs me, to think that someone could push me out of my own home," lamented Harriett.

She sat silently until they arrived at the same steakhouse where they had dinner a few nights ago. They entered the restaurant and were seated at a table for two. The server placed menus on the table, and George and Harriett each ordered coffee.

"What are we going to do, George? I am a little freaked out that someone has entered my place, gone through my things, and to top it all off, put cameras and recording devices in my place."

"I'm sorry, Harriett, that you are caught up in this," consoled George as he took her trembling hands in his and gently rubbed them. He gave them a little squeeze. His eyes conveyed his deep concern and, perhaps, much deeper feelings for her. "Do you want to go to your dad's now?"

"No, I do not want to leave you with this. I will be all right. Now, I am starting to get angry. Let us work on this together, because like it or not, they have dragged me into this foray. I will not run away!" declared Harriett.

"Good girl!" exclaimed George. "We will get through this. How is your prayer life?"

With that question, Harriett chuckled, and looking more relaxed, she said, "Well, since that incident at the river, I pray all the time. Jesus and I are very good friends. We talk and laugh a lot together. I love Him so very much!"

A fit of laughter enveloped Harriett as tension and stress gave way to peace and strength. Harriett dabbed her eyes, noticing that George too was laughing as hard as she was.

"Oh, my side hurts!" exclaimed Harriett, holding onto her side.

"Mine does too," said George.

The euphoric air of laughter was receding as they laughed themselves out. A peace and calmness settled over them, and they sat in compatible silence, drinking their coffee. Soon, their food was served, and they found that they were hungrier than they thought. The food was delicious and they devoured it with fervency. Another cup of coffee and a piece of apple pie topped off the excellent meal.

"You know, George, those people know that we know that my apartment has been bugged. Why don't we go back to my place and take the cameras and mics and just get rid of them?"

"I think that would be a good plan. However, we do not know if there are more surveillance devices in there." George paused. "I am going to call my lawyer. See if we can go see him." George pulled out his cell phone and placed the call and James agreed to meet them.

After George hung up, he said to Harriett, "Come on, let us go. I want to go back to your place and get those devices to take with us."

Harriett rose and put on her jacket. She grabbed her purse and slung it over her shoulder as George paid the bill. Leaving the restaurant, they did not notice a man rise from another table and follow them out the door.

When George and Harriett arrived at James's office, George introduced Harriett to him.

"I know your dad, Harriett. I worked for him for a couple of summers. You were just little at the time. It is nice to meet again. How is your dad? I was sorry to hear about your mother's passing. She was such a kind and sweet lady," said James as he motioned for them to be seated.

"Oh, thank you, Mr. Lewis. But I am sorry I do not remember you," said Harriett.

"Well, you were young at the time. Now, George, my detective has been very busy. Here is his report. Read and initial it; then we can discuss it further."

George read the report. He was shocked to see some names that he recognized. He initiated the document and handed it back to James.

"There are events happening with some very dangerous and nasty people, George. How they got you mixed up in this is a mystery. It seems as if there is a lot of corporate espionage going on. But that is not the crux of it. There are rumors of terrorism and foreign infiltration in certain companies around the country.

"The federal and state police as well as military investigators are working together to expose the infiltrators. But there are more and more cyberattacks getting through some of the most sophisticated and secure firewalls in the country. Many companies are tightening up on their hiring policies. For all that, there is only so much that one can do in background checks. Some of the issues are coming through subcontracted workers. These are the people whom employers such as yourself have nothing to do with. For instance, you hire a janitorial company, they hire people, subcontractors, to come in and perform janitorial duties. You are relying on the janitorial company to hire good people. Little do they know, or maybe they do know, that the people they are hiring are terrorists. This can lead to a quagmire of mistrust, misunderstanding, and mistakes that could take years to sort out and correct. In the meantime, many good people will lose their businesses, their livelihoods, their families . . . What I do not understand is, why are you being targeted? You are a new company. This does not make sense."

George had been pondering the same thing. Nothing about this makes any sense at all. Who and why would anyone be interested in a small engineering firm like his? Questions, questions, always more questions, and no feasible answers.

Chapter 16

The names on the report had piqued George's curiosity. He remembered Herbert Hubbard from his days in university. He had sat in on a couple of his sessions and attended a rally that Hubbard had spoken at. George never liked the man's politics. Hubbard was too far left wing. He did not know Jack Lang nor Millie Middleton from the University of Central City. However, George did remember Jonathan Weather, a professor of economics at the University of Orion. George had taken two economic classes from him. He liked Jonathan Weathers, for he was smart and a very good instructor. George knew that politically, Jonathan Weathers leaned to the left, but he never pushed his beliefs on anyone, so it surprised George to see his name on this report. The report also revealed a little-known group called the Brotherhood of Theoretical Economic and Political Sciences. Since he left university, George had not heard about, much less thought about them.

George relayed that he knew several of the people on the report and explained to James how and when he knew them and what he knew about them.

Then came the last part of the report. Vince White, head of the Last Stronghold of Rights and Freedoms, made George's hair stand on end. Oh yes, he recognized that name!

"The one I know is the most dangerous to me is Vince White. We went to university together. We were competing on a project, and I won the competition. Vince could not take the defeat and he looked at it as an insult. Vince is very shrewd but extremely vindictive. He is also a bully and a narcissist. He bullied his team so badly that all but one walked out on him. He blames everyone but himself for his failures, and if he is caught up in this thing, then he has matured into a dangerous hateful person.

"When I was in my fifth year of university, I had been approached by Vince and a couple of his friends," continued George. "They had effectively boxed me in a triangle. Then Vince and his friends started taunting me. When they could not get a rise out of me, they closed in more. I knew that I was in extreme danger. Vince wanted to fight; I could sense it. He turned as if to walk away when he suddenly lunged at me. But I stepped aside and backhanded him, catching him in the face. Vince's forward momentum and failure to connect with me caused him to lose his balance and fall forward. Vince landed face first, smashing onto the concrete, resulting in a bloody broken nose and two knocked out teeth. As Vince managed to lift his head, he said to me, 'This ain't over, Hamer. I will get you if it is the last thing I do!'

"Quickly glancing back, I saw pure hatred in Vince's eyes. I absolutely hate altercations and violence. I would rather be a peacemaker. However, I am not afraid to fight and defend myself or someone else if I must. I knew that these guys would have killed me; I knew they had murder on their minds and in their hearts. I found out later that Vince had hired a fellow to ingratiate himself into our group at university and he drugged me, almost costing me my life."

As George recalled this altercation, he could still feel the palpable hatred of Vince and it made his skin feel as though stinging ants were squirming and biting him. Was Vince responsible for the security breaches in his company? Was Vince responsible for what happened to Scott? Again, so many questions with no answers.

James took the documents back from George and placed them in a file folder. He took his glasses off and looked squarely at him.

"This man is dangerous, George. However, there is one who is even more dangerous. His name is Jacob Weiss. Have you heard of the Last Stronghold of Rights and Freedoms?"

"No, not really. When I was in university, there was a new group starting up called Preservation of Our Rights and Freedoms. Is this the same thing?"

"A few years ago, there were several small groups, such as the one you mentioned, starting up on campuses all over the country, but they all fizzled out. That is, until Jacob Weiss entered the scene. He came from Hungary. This man is extraordinarily smart, a real genius. He is also very sly. He puts on a good facade, but under that facade is a devil. He is very good at manipulating people and masterminding events for his own agenda. Even though he does not hold a degree in psychology, he is well trained in the understanding of the human psyche, which he uses to his full advantage.

"So, it will come as no surprise that he is the top kingpin of the Brotherhood of the Last Stronghold of Rights and Freedoms. Jacob Weiss is a very, very dangerous man. The real goal of this man and his cohorts is world domination. You may think that this is impossible, but let me assure you that you are wrong. There are evil forces working together to accomplish all of this. These people will stop at nothing to obtain their goal. They will set things up in such a way that people will rally around them, thinking that they are indeed defending rights and freedoms—but they are being deceived. So, when someone begins to see the deceptions and questions it or talks against it, they vanish as if that person never existed. I tell you, George, these are dangerous, dangerous people." James leaned back in his chair and drew in a deep breath, waiting for George to assimilate and digest what he just heard.

"How many other businesses are being affected around here?"

"There are some others that have had security breaches over the past thirty-six hours," responded James. "The police have finished up at your office, and you can go back now. I have set it up with my IT team to work with your team to get your system up and running.

"Mitchell is over there now. We want to make sure there are no Trojans or other hidden viruses planted in your system. I know that the cyber team from the police department is extremely good, but right now, there are few technicians I trust."

"That is good news. This means that my assets and bank accounts are no longer frozen?" asked George.

"Yes, everything and everybody has been checked out. But there is some question about Scott. I know that he is in the hospital very badly hurt. Now I cannot verify this, but it has been suggested that he has been attending some of these rallies over in Central City. See if you can find out what he knows. He must know something to have been beaten this badly. Oh, by the way, I had someone sweep your hotel room and Harriett's apartment; we found some surveillance bugs and cameras. Your room is clean now, and so is Harriett's apartment. I would suggest that you leave the hotel and rent yourself an apartment until your house is repaired. The repair work cannot start until the police are finished with their investigation, which, of course, could take a few more weeks."

"Thanks, James, I will see what I can do about Scott and I will see about renting an apartment," said George as he got up from his chair. "I am going over to the hospital now. Scott should be out of recovery. Thanks again."

Chapter 17

At the hospital, George and Harriett went up to the ICU. When they reached the nurses' station, alarms started ringing. The nurse who was helping George and Harriett quickly excused herself and dashed away. George and Harriett were left in wonderment. Concern and a sick feeling caused George's stomach to turn. Thinking that this emergency could be Scott taking a turn for the worse, George started praying in the Spirit. Harriett joined George and started praying in the Spirit too.

Taking George's hand, Harriett led him to the waiting room, to a place where they could sit. George sat down while Harriett went to the water cooler and got a cup of water. She returned to where George was sitting and handed him the cone-shaped cup.

George looked up at her with anguish and said, "I really hope that wasn't Scott." George took the cup of water and drank it.

"Mr. Hamer?" called a nurse as she came to the waiting room.

"Yes?" replied George, getting up from the couch.

"You can come and see your friend now."

"Is he okay?" asked George.

"Oh, yes," replied the nurse. "Scott is awake now, so you can come in, but you can only see him for a few minutes."

George and Harriett entered Scott's room to find his hands and torso heavily bandaged. His eyes were so swollen, they had become slits in his extremely bruised face. George put his hand gently on Scott's shoulder. He drew in a deep breath to calm himself.

"Hey, buddy," said George softly. "Just wanted you to know that I am here. You remember Harriett?"

Scott glanced over to Harriett but quickly fixed his eyes back onto George. He started to say something, but George interrupted him, realizing that Scott was not in any condition to speak as his jaws were wired shut.

"It is okay, Scott. Do not try to talk right now. Whatever it is, we can talk when you are stronger."

Scott seemed to relax, and his eyes closed as he drifted off to sleep. Just then, the nurse came in. "You'll have to leave now," she said.

George and Harriett quietly left the room. They stopped again at the nurses' station, as the doctor was there going over Scott's chart.

"Doctor," George started, "how is Scott doing, really?"

The doctor finished reading Scott's chart before answering.

"The surgery went well. Scott is young and otherwise in very good health. He will be here in the ICU for another day or two, and then transferred to a ward for a few more days. You can come and see him again tomorrow."

"Okay, thank you, Doctor," said George.

As George and Harriett were driving to George's firm, they talked about Scott and the long haul of more surgery and recovery that was facing him.

"I sure hope that Scott will have use of his hands after surgery," commented George.

"We'll be praying for healing over him," said Harriett. "He is in God's hands. He will recover."

They arrived at the office and found Chief Commander Schultz sitting in George's chair.

"Chief Commander Schultz! What are you doing here? I understand that your investigation is over and that I can open for business again."

"Yes, yes, what you are saying is quite true. I noticed that your IT guy and some others—people from your lawyer's office, I take it—have been in here going through your computer system."

"Yeah, so?" queried George a little disdainfully.

I have one little question for you, if you do not mind?"

"Go ahead, what is your question?"

"Do you recognize this man?" asked Schultz as he took a photo out of an envelope and handed it to George.

George took the photo. After looking at it, he said, "Yes, I know this guy. What of it?"

"So, this man you do know. Who is he? How do you know him?"

"Why do you want to know?" asked George, who was tired of questions and all the prying that had been done not only to his business, but also his personal life.

"Please, Mr. Hamer, I am just doing my job. Please tell me how you know him? And tell me also if you know this man," said Schultz as he handed another photo to George.

George looked at the second picture and said, "I do not know him, but I have seen him before. Who is he?"

"Please tell me about the first man," instructed Schultz.

"His name is Vince White. He and I attended the same university."

Chief Commander Schultz looked at George, studying his mannerism and face before continuing, "And this second man, you do not know but have seen him before. Is this correct?"

"Yes," said George, still hesitant to reveal where he had seen him before.

"Come, come, Mr. Hamer, I know about the video," said Schultz.

"I need to call my lawyer. In fact, I will do that right now."

"Never mind," said Schultz. "I'll let myself out."

George and Harriett followed Chief Commander Schultz to the front doors and watched him leave the premises.

"I need to get a locksmith in here and change all the locks. Can you believe that guy!"

"I see one problem," Harriett as she and George returned to his office. "Chief Commander Schultz may have told us who that guy is."

"I know who he is," said a voice from behind them.

Both George and Harriett jumped at the sound. George turned around. "Mitchell! I did not know anyone was here!"

"Sorry, Boss, did not mean to startle you. That guy's name is Mikhail Crusikoff, and he is with the Russian Mafia," explained Mitchell as he sat down across from George.

"How do you know this stuff?" asked George incredulously.

"When all of this happened, I started to do some investigating myself. So, I broke into some top-secret places at the Russian Embassy in Washington."

"Weren't you afraid of getting caught?" asked Harriett.

"No. I use a computer that leaves no footprints at all; I developed it myself. It cannot be traced in any way or form. So, I went through the embassy computer, into their secret service—this Mikhail is an operative working for the Russian government, operating through the Mafia. I am telling you these guys are no joke."

"Wow, Mitchell! I did not know you could develop your own computer system like that!" exclaimed George. He looked closely at Mitchell.

"Mitchell, why are you working for me? My company is not what you need. You need to be in Silicon Valley or one of those companies that would promote you and help you develop your creations."

"Well, Boss, there are a couple of reasons. First off, I had a job in Silicon Valley, a very junior position. But, as I watched and learned, I knew that I would never belong there. It is hard to explain, but I will try. Those people see nothing before them except money and power in the cyberworld. Much of their work would be good for mankind, but they are not interested in the welfare of mankind. Do not get me wrong, wonderful technology—useful in many areas of life–has come out of the Valley. But believe it or not, that type of technology is but a byproduct of the deeper technology they are developing. Plus, the byproducts fund their true functions. There is big, big money up for grabs. The geniuses developing and building these systems are not necessarily interested in just the big bucks, but are more interested in seeing how far and wide they can delve into cyberspace, creating and developing smarter and smarter mega computer systems.

"It is the people behind the people who truly want total control and domination over all of mankind and the Earth. I want no part of any of that. Do you know that I am a Christian? I believe in the creation of the world and universe. I believe everything that Jesus said and did. I follow Him. He has gifted me with the intelligence to do the things I do. Do you know that He led me to you? It was not a coincidence that I was hired by you. This is the reason I have been so upset about what has happened to you. So, I tried to fix it. Perhaps I should not have breached the firewalls of the Russian Foreign office or of their embassy in Washington. I was desperate to help you. I do not like doing things like that. It can be intoxicating, knowing that you can slip in and out of systems without leaving a trace. I have already repented of this action. I will not do it again. It is just too easy." Mitchell finished his explanation and sat quietly as George and Harriett digested what he said.

"Thank you, Mitchell," said George. "This information is helpful. I will share what you have learned with my lawyer. His detective is doing his own investigation."

"Mitchell," began Harriett, "do you know what Vince White's involvement is in all of this?"

"Oh, yes, I nearly forgot to tell you, George. Vince White is up to his eyeballs in all of this. He is an operative of the Russian government. He is low-level right now, but it looks as though he may be promoted up through the ranks soon. But that is all I know right now," answered Mitchell. "By the way, how is Scott?"

George's eyes flicked from Harriett back to Mitchell. "He is doing okay. He survived surgery and is in the ICU. They say that he will need surgery on his hands too. Seeing as you are here, Mitchell, will you send emails to all our employees and tell them that we will be open for business tomorrow? I want to get everything back to normal as soon as possible. We still have deadlines to meet. Thanks, Mitchell."

"I am on it, Boss. It will be good to get everything back to normal."

Chapter 18

The next morning, all of George's employees were at their desks, chatting happily as they organized their day. George stopped by each department to welcome everyone back.

"I want to thank all of you for hanging in there with me. I also want to assure everyone that you will receive your full pay as usual. We are now behind on all our projects. The major one is now almost four months behind and must be caught up. I would appreciate it if you all could handle working an extra hour or so each day until we are caught up.

"As you know, Scott is in the hospital with severe injuries due to a cruel beating. I cannot go into any details about that, mainly because I do not know, but there is an investigation being conducted. Scott was lead for the Three Valley Mining project. I have asked Dale Withers to step in and take over. So, those of you who are working on this project, be advised that Dale is your go-to supervisor. I also want to introduce a new employee. This is Harriett Baird. Harriett is a well-qualified engineer and graduated from the Bantine University, with a major in engineering and minor in music. She has been working for a firm out West. Many of you would know her family as they have lived in this area for many years."

"Thank you, George," began Harriett. "I am so happy to be back in Crescent River. I do see some familiar faces. Crescent River has grown so much over the past several years; I look forward to working with everyone."

"Harriett will be working on a new project that we had bid on just before this fiasco had happened," said George. "I know that you will assist her as she gets settled in. I will be going over to the hospital a little later and will keep everyone informed regarding Scott's progress. Well, let us get back to work."

Later that afternoon, George headed over to the hospital to find Scott sitting up in bed.

"I must say, Scott, you look horrible. You look like you have been through a meat grinder." George smiled at his friend.

"Yeah, I bet I do." Scott chuckled with his jaws wired shut and face still swollen. He did his best to keep up the well-meaning banter. "It is good to see you, George."

"Hey, man, you know I am always here for you. Can you tell me what happened and why?" George pulled a chair closer to Scott's bed and sat down.

"George, I am so sorry about what happened. I tried to stop it. I really did! By the time, I found out what these guys were up to it was too late. These guys are truly evil and extremely dangerous. The information they were given concerning you was total fabrication. You were not supposed to be the target. Do you remember Vince White, from our days at university? Well, he is behind all of this. He is heavily involved with this group. I only know this because a friend of mine had been involved until she found out their true motives. So, I thought I could go and reason with the head guy. All I got for my efforts was this severe beating. They were going to kill me. I am surprised they did not kill me. The last thing I heard was someone saying that Vince White is dead meat. Next thing I knew, I was here." Scott sank back into his pillow as fatigue started to settle in his muscles and he fell asleep.

George left Scott and headed to his lawyer's office. On his way, he pondered Scott's words, wondering how anyone could be so devious and so full of hatred that they would do such a thing.

"Hey, James," greeted George as he entered James's office. "Thanks for seeing me."

"Come in, George; have a seat," invited James. "What is on your mind? I take it everyone is back to work."

"Yes, everyone came in this morning. Thank you for getting everything done. I know you pulled some strings to get everyone's money released and cell phones back to them. Mitchell has already scanned their phones for any tracking devices and that sort of thing, but they all checked out clean. Now I have a couple of issues to discuss with you. First off, I went to see Scott, in fact, what he has told me shocks me," said George.

"Hold on a minute, George. Mildred, would you bring your steno pad and a recorder in please," requested James through his intercom.

Mildred, a middle-aged woman, neatly groomed and rather striking with her graying hair and straight posture, entered quietly and placed the recorder on James's desk and took a seat off to George's right.

George then relayed the entire conversation that he had just had with Scott. He left out nothing.

"Oh, my God!" exclaimed James. "That fills in a lot of blanks. I am going to put on some security for Scott. I do not believe he is out of the woods yet. They may try again. I will get my detective on it right away. Now, George, you said you had a couple of things. What else?"

George explained to James what Mitchell had done, leaving out none of the details.

"So, you see, James, I do not want anything to happen to Mitchell. He has been very loyal and very helpful."

"There could be ramifications from this if the feds find out. That is on the business side. What bothers me even more is this matter of breaking into an embassy and into another country's secret service computer system. If these backfires and somehow a trace is found, Mitchell could be charged with espionage and his life could even be in more danger. Mistakes can happen. Always be prepared for the unexpected. Going back to the business side, it is going to be very difficult to explain how suddenly, all your files are back on your computer."

"I never thought of that," said George. "The files have already been downloaded into our main frame. Mitchell refurbished the main frames last night and downloaded everything early this morning. He worked all night on it."

"Well, there may be a way," said James. "They didn't happen to ask you if you had any other computers other than the ones you showed them, did they?"

"No . . . no, they didn't," answered George. "Why?"

"It's really no one's business if you keep files at another location. It happens frequently. The tricky part is that it does make it fraud if the IRS shows that two sets of files are available and do not match each other. Now that Mitchell has downloaded all the files, he must somehow get rid of any lingering telltales that speak of a separate system. You see, what is going to happen is that in a few months, the feds are going to demand an audit and require you to send them reports on the past three to six months of work. They may send some agents, or they may just send you a demand letter. Either way, this will be tricky. I would suggest that you be proactive and let them know that you had a backup system over and above the system that was corrupted. They can come and go over your books. You do not have anything to hide because you have not done anything wrong. Now, the downside of that is they may find one of your computers that was used in this disaster. Questions will be raised. Some very hard questions. Although, I do not see how that could happen. The data saved would be only that which is entered in and saved. No unsaved data would be backed up.

"Mildred, get a hold of Paul for me and have him come see me as soon as possible.

"I know what you want to do now, George. You want to go back to your office so that you and Mitchell can go over all the activities done over the last several weeks to see if you can find out which computer it was that all this started from. Let this go. Let the feds decide what they want to do. If they come in and find it when they do the audit, then it becomes their problem. It would be easier for you to defend. So, I have your word that you will not do that?"

George gritted his teeth because this is exactly what he wanted to do. He sat for a moment, then gave his word that he would not do that.

"Okay, George. I am doing this to protect you and your firm. I believe that you will do what I have asked of you. You are one of the very few honorable men in business, so I will trust you."

"Thanks, James. I really will do what you have asked. I have always lived my life as my word is my bond," said George. He rose from his chair, shook hands with his lawyer, and left his office.

George returned to his office and went to find Mitchell, who was deep in his computer lab, reading screens, scanning information, and doing whatever computer geeks do to keep the computer systems up and running. There were also two other IT guys working on the computers as well.

"Hey, Mitchell," said George as he stood behind Mitchell, looking at rows and rows of numbers, letters, dots, and dashes all scrolling endlessly on the screen.

"Oh, hi, Boss, how's it going?" said Mitchell as he stood up.

"Need to speak with you. Let us go into your office," said George.

Mitchell poured himself and George each a cup of coffee from his coffee maker.

"I just got back from my lawyer's office," said George. "I have a question about these files that are saved to your computer. Is it possible for you to tell which computer was used? I am not saying it was an inside job. I do not believe it was. But just suppose that all of this came through one of our office computers, and if so, which one? Can you tell?"

Mitchell thought for a moment and responded, "Look at this screen, Boss. This is your computer being downloaded now. You can see the work that you were doing. Everything that you entered is recorded. I have gone through all the data saved, and I could not find anything unusual on anyone's computer. I last backed everything up on Tuesday at five thirty p.m. The Trojan and the unauthorized download happened somewhere around two thirty Wednesday morning. The download did not actually happen because I put into the system a program designed to thwart any unauthorized download after midnight. I told nobody about that extra piece of security so that when a crash happens, whoever is responsible is left empty-handed. Our data is secure right now.

"In answer to your question, no, there is no way to tell if any of this was done from an inside computer. All I can say is, nothing was set up before Tuesday afternoon. And another thing, the federal experts could not find any indication of an inside breach. Those guys have access to the most sophisticated equipment and technology in the world. If they could not find the breach, it either doesn't exist or there is someone with much better technology. There is one other thing, though; I have not seen it, just heard about it. A European company has a technology that can be used off site. Without being on site, they can get into a computer and cause all kinds of havoc. There is one catch, though: someone must put a USB into a computer port. The USB can be designed to release information into that specific computer on a timed basis. But then, someone must come back in and remove the USB. Did not happen here because we were all here first thing in the morning and no authorized or unauthorized entry was recorded after three a.m. Wednesday, and no unauthorized USB ports were found here. I know because I checked."

George sat quietly for a moment contemplating what he had heard. He finished the last of his coffee and rose to his feet. He placed his cup on the table and said to Mitchell, "Okay then. Sounds as though we can carry on and move forward. I was told, though, that the IRS will want full financial reports in three to six months. That is when they will find out that your system is intact. Well, we will face that when it comes. Thanks, Mitchell, for all your help. Catch up with you later."

Chapter 19

The rest of the week went well, and everything was gradually returning to normal. Work orders were coming in on jobs that had been bid on. Catch-up work was progressing quickly and smoothly.

A few more weeks passed, and George's house was finished and brand-new furniture and appliances were delivered and installed. His cheques from the insurance company for the renovations and the business losses arrived and were safely deposited into the appropriate accounts.

"Harriett," said George as he popped into her office. "I am going over to the hospital to pick up Scott. He is being released today. I will be back in a little while. Maybe we can take Scott for lunch. I want to talk to him once more. Do you want to meet us at Tiny Tim's at noon?"

"Sure," replied Harriett. "But do you really want me there? Scott may not feel comfortable around me." Harriett closed her laptop and gazed up at George. She had fallen in love with him. She never imagined she would experience such deep emotions.

"Of course, I want you to come with me, Harriett. Scott has always trusted my judgments. He will learn to trust you, and besides, he knows that I would not approach sensitive issues with him unless I knew and trusted the person I brought with me," responded George. "You are my right arm. I will always want you with me." He winked at Harriett and left her office.

Harriett smiled to herself and, with the giddiness born of love and acceptance, returned to her work with enthusiasm.

***

George arrived at the hospital and went to Scott's room to find two police officers in there speaking to him.

"As we have mentioned, Mr. McDonald, we have a body in the police morgue. We need you to come and see if you can identify it," said Sergeant O'Malley.

"George is coming to pick me up. I will see if he can take me to the morgue, but I do not see how I can help. Oh, here is George now," said Scott. "George, the police have found a body. I need to go to the morgue."

"Hello, Sergeant O'Malley. Do you know whose body it might be?" asked George.

"Not a hundred percent. The body has been in the water a while. We are running fingerprints now," explained Sergeant O'Malley.

"Okay, we'll come as soon as Scott is discharged," said George.

Sergeant O'Malley was satisfied with that and left.

"How are your hands, Scott?"

George observed Scott's well bandaged hands and wondered how he was going to manage at home on his own.

"They are doing very well. The doctor is supposed to remove these bandages before I leave. They will fit me with some flexible gloves. I was expecting the doctor a couple of hours ago. Guess an emergency or something has come up. The nurse just let me know a few minutes ago that the doctor is on his way now. Should be here soon. The stitches will be removed today. Will have to go for physiotherapy as well," chattered Scott.

George could hear the tension and stress in Scott's voice. "What is it about this body that the cops want you to come to the morgue?"

"I do not really know. They think that this guy is mixed up with what happened to you and me," explained Scott as some of the tension left his voice. "But I really do not know anything. I cannot identify the guys who did this to me. Their faces were masked. I might recognize voices, but I doubt that too. I was in too much pain."

A half hour later, the doctor and a nurse came into Scott's room. As they were pulling the privacy curtains around Scott's bed, the nurse said to George, "I am sorry, sir, but you cannot be in here. There is a waiting room just down the hall. I will let you know when we are done and Mr. McDonald can be taken home."

George was somewhat relieved to leave the room. He did not really want to see what the doctor and nurse were going to be doing. George wandered down the hall and sat down to wait. He picked up a newspaper and read it from front to back. Nothing too interesting there. He thumbed through some magazines unable to focus on any of the articles. Finally, he put everything down and just watched people coming and going, up and down the hallway. George's mind was racing over all the events that had led to this moment. He had not yet had the heart or desire to question Scott about the letter he wrote to him. Again, questions, questions, and more questions with no answers or solutions in sight. George sighed and stood to stretch his legs just as the nurse came in with Scott in tow.

"I'm ready to go, George," said Scott. "Actually, more than ready to go."

The nurse left Scott with George and went on her way.

"Okay, buddy, let's vacate this popsicle stand," said George with relief. He looked at the flexible gloves covering Scott's hands. They were quite nice. Made of blue nylon and spandex, they fit snuggly but not tightly over his fingers and hands. They were not bulky but had some padding to protect against bumps and bangs.

"How long will you have to wear these gloves, Scott?

"Just a few weeks. My hands are healing nicely, they say. I will be starting physio next week. The treatments will go on for the next six to twelve weeks, depending on how I progress. At least, the pain is pretty much gone now. I can move my fingers some. I am grateful to the doctors and nurses for their care, but I am most grateful to you, George. You saved my life. Thank you for standing with me and helping with all these medical expenses. I am looking forward to coming back to work."

They left the hospital and arrived at George's parked car.

"Of course, my friend and brother," said George as he opened the car door for Scott. "We will talk more about that later. Let us go for lunch. Would you like to go to Tiny Tim's? They have renovated it since the last time you were there. It is very nice, but still with that homey atmosphere. Food is as good as ever."

Scott nodded his head, and George closed the door and walked around to the driver's side and got in. He started the Camaro and smiled at the roar of the engine as it came to life.

"Ah, George? Did you forget that I must go to the police morgue?"

"Oh, yeah, guess I did forget for a moment. Maybe we should do that first and get it out of the way," responded George.

At the morgue, the men met up with Sergeant O'Malley. He led them down to the viewing room.

"Now remember, this guy has been in the water for a spell and some fish have chewed on him. He has been fixed up the best we could do," explained O'Malley as he pulled back the curtain.

Both George and Scott gasped at the sight. There on the table lay the decomposing body of Vince White.

Chapter 20

There was no mistaking him. Being dead did not enhance Vince White's looks in any way.

"I see that you two know him," observed O'Malley. "Who is he and how do you know him?"

George answered, "His name is Vince White. We went to university together."

Scott piped up, "He was the one who set up the guy that spiked George's drink, which almost cost George his life back when we were at university."

"What else do you know about him?" asked O'Malley, watching both George and Scott carefully.

Scott continued to stare at the body on the other side of the window and chose not to say anything else.

"Are you both sure that you know nothing else? You know it is a federal offense to keep information from an ongoing investigation?"

Scott refused to say anything else. Sergeant O'Malley sighed, realizing that these two men were going to stay silent. "Okay, you two can leave now. But I will probably be coming to question you further."

"If you think you have to, then go and see our lawyer," said George as he and Scott left the viewing room and then exited the building.

As George and Scott got into George's car, George pulled out his cell phone and called James Lewis to let him know they were coming to talk.

"Listen, Scott, we must get to the bottom of all this. You are going to tell James everything. And I mean everything."

Scott nodded his head in agreement. However, he was not looking forward to it. George was right, he needed to get this all off his chest.

Within minutes, George and Scott were seated in James's office, along with his secretary. "Okay, why were you at the police morgue? You should have called me right away, George."

"Well, they told Scott to come. Seeing as I am driving him, I took him there and went in with him," replied George. "Now, what I want is for Scott to fill you and me in on the events that have led to the attack of my business and home."

"Okay, let's get started with the question, why, Scott, did the police have you come to the police morgue and who was it that you were to identify?" questioned James. He signaled to his secretary to start recording the conversation.

"Okay," said Scott. "The body at the morgue is Vince White. He was shot execution style according to the officers that saw me in the hospital, and then thrown into the river. Of course, someone found it, and the police came to see me in the hospital and told me to identify the body. It was Vince, who got someone to spike George's beer. You see, Vince was extremely jealous of George and hated him with an obsessive hatred. But Vince was not done with George. He was heavily involved with the Brotherhood for Preservation of Our Rights. He came up through the ranks until he became the grand master, but this group is only a small sect of a larger one. A big promotion was coming for him and would give him almost unlimited power."

Scott paused, looked at George as if there was something more he wanted to say, but thought better of it.

"When I became fully aware of all that was happening to you, George, I did some investigating and came across a low-level guy in the organization. He told me everything I needed to know. So, I thought I could handle the situation and bring everything to a close. I did not want to worry you, George. I really did try to fix this thing. I am sorry. I should have given you a heads-up, but I really believed that I was doing the right thing and I thought I could put a stop to it before things went too far. But as you can see, I was wrong." Scott leaned back in his chair before continuing. He accepted a glass of water being offered. He took a long drink, then continued with his story.

"I approached a man named Heinrich Gruberfink. I was told that he was Jacob Weiss's henchman. I told him who I was and that I had vital information that could only be told to Jacob Weiss, himself. I finally convinced Heinrich to let me see Jacob. Two days later, I was taken from the street. My head was covered with a hood, and my hands were bound. I was shoved into a van and driven away. I was taken out from the back of the van and led up a trail then up a few steps to a door. Someone knocked on the door, and it opened and we went inside. The hood was removed from my head. All I saw was a very dimly lit windowless room. They shone a narrow bright light in my eyes and pushed me onto a hard wooden chair. A gravelly heavily accented voice asked for the information that I said I had. I told him that George Hamer was not the man they were told about. I explained to him that George had just started up his business, that George had no political associations with anyone other than the usual Republican or Democratic parties. He had no connections with the Secret Services, or any other federal intelligence agencies. The misinformation that they had on George was purely made up by Vince White. They had asked if I could prove it. I told them to check out a source in Vince's old group. I gave them the name. They gave me a drink of water. Next thing I remember is that I was at home."

Scott looked around at George and James, waiting for a reproof or something equally unpleasant but deserved.

"I thought my investigator did a good job!" exclaimed James. "That was nothing compared to what you have said, Scott. But your story fills in the holes that my investigator could not fill. Was it these guys that did all this damage to you?"

"No, this is all thanks to Vince White and his goons because I overheard one of the goons say that Vince will be pleased when they finish me off," answered Scott, looking down at his hands. "I was not surprised to see his body. Now, though, George, everything should come back to normal for you."

George looked closely at Scott, marveling that he was still alive. Then George turned his attention to James and said, "James, what should we do with this information? The police will want all this for their investigations."

"We do nothing with it. This is way too much to pass over to the local authorities, or even the state authorities."

"James is right, George," interjected Scott. "These issues go right to the top. We can take no chances, at least not yet. We must be very careful from here on in."

"I don't understand," said George quizzically.

"George, all I want to do is heal, get back to work, and forget about all of this stuff."

"Scott is right, George. We will put ourselves and this whole community into jeopardy if we do anything at the present time. A time will come when we will have to step forward, but until we can be sure of whom we can trust, we say nothing. Okay? Right?"

George, again, looked at each man and acquiesced but was not happy about it. George had a nagging question that needed an answer.

"Who was the man that breached my computer security? The man I saw go into the mobster's tavern, the same man who bugged Harriett's apartment? Does anyone know?"

"What did he look like?" asked Scott.

"He was around six feet, blonde hair, blue eyes, sharp features," replied George, pulling on his memory.

"That sounds like Heinrich Gruberfink. When was the last time you saw him?"

"Last time was when I lost him in an alley when I was chasing him. He had come out of Harriett's building then," replied George.

"He is not only Jacob's henchman but also a top-notch computer scientist, a go-between for the Russian mob and the elitists, of which Jacob is one of them. He does not take kindly to the blunderings of people whom he feels are inferior to himself. Has more than likely filled any holes in this operation. If he has not yet, he will. He really is a very dangerous man. George, you were lucky that you did not catch up to him. You may not have survived the encounter," explained Scott.

George took in all the information, putting each piece into a mental compartment for later examination. However, he was relieved that all of this was over and that Scott survived the ordeal and was on his way to total recovery. George breathed a sigh of relief and said a quiet prayer of thanks to God.

Chapter 21

Lunchtime found George and Scott at Tiny Tim's.
"Harriett was supposed to meet us here," said George a bit wistfully. "She just texted to say she won't be able to come after all." George put his phone back into his pocket and turned his attention to the waitress.

George and Scott ordered their meals and sat back to enjoy a cup of coffee until their meals arrived. Chatting casually and laughing at some silly things, they failed to see that Harriett and a strange man were sitting in a booth at the back of the restaurant.

The server came with George's and Scott's meals and set the plates down when suddenly a loud ruckus broke out a few tables away. Everyone could hear the resounding sound of a slap and a deep breath being drawn in. George turned in his booth. Shock quickly turned to acute anger as he saw Harriett's reddened face and tears in her eyes. Jumping up, without thought or reason, George had the assailant by the collar of his jacket and hoisted him out of his chair. Still gripping the startled man and with one more giant step, he shoved the man out the restaurant door.

"You ever, ever come near Harriett again, much less lay so much as a little finger on her, I'll break every bone in your body," threatened George through clenched teeth. "Now get out of here and don't ever come back."

The man, who was short but muscular, straightened himself up and glared at the tall, well-built man with blazing eyes standing before him, and then decided to walk away.

George went back into the restaurant, and all the patrons clapped their hands in appreciation. The server had given Harriett a cold cloth for her face. Harriett wished that the floor would open and swallow her. George helped Harriett out of her chair and gently led her over to his table. Harriett slid into the booth, and George sat down next to her. He looked tenderly at her and took her trembling hand into his warm one.

The server brought a pot of tea and set it before Harriett. She lifted the cup, but she was still shaking so that the tea slopped. Putting the cup down, Harriett said, "I . . I want to go home."

"Okay, I'll take you," said George, and he waved for the server. "Scott, do you want me to take you home first, or do you want to come with us, to Harriett's?"

"Think I will just go home, George. Harriett, I am sorry about this. Listen, I am only a phone call away. I can help you if you want," said Scott compassionately.

"Thanks, Scott. How are you doing, by the way? I did not even ask. Do you need anything?" asked Harriett in gratitude to both men for not asking impossible questions, questions that she was not ready to answer.

"No, I will be fine. I have a housekeeper coming in to clean and I can order take-out food. I will make out fine," replied Scott.

***

After arriving at Scott's place, George checked around, making sure that everything was okay on the inside. He also checked around the back and the garage. Scott, in the meantime, stepped into the house and a shudder passed through his body as the remembrance of what had happened washed over him. He could see that George had made sure that all the blood and other damages that had been done were cleaned and repaired. The house had lost the air of safety and security. It was as if the house was in mourning and it no longer belonged to Scott.

As Scott wandered through the house, room by room, the oppressiveness grew heavier and heavier. Scott hurried outside just as George was pulling out of the driveway. George spied Scott and stopped. Scott caught up to the car as George stopped and got out.

"I have changed my mind, George. I will come with you," said Scott.

George opened the back door and Scott got in.

"You okay, Scott?" inquired Harriett.

"No, not really. I cannot stay there. I think I will sell my place, lock, stock, and barrel. I will never belong there again." Scott sank back into the seat and closed his eyes.

***

As George pulled away from the curb, Harriett glanced back at Scott, her heart aching for the damage that was done to him. Not just physical, but emotional and spiritual as well. She turned her gaze to George. She loved him. She loved everything about him—his courage, his strength, his empathy, and most of all his tenderness and gentleness. For such a big man, he was incredibly gentle. She felt safe with him.

"I'll take you home first, Harriett," said George with a hint of regret. "Then I'll drop Scott off at my place. I need to go back to the office and finish up some work."

"Okay," said Harriett in agreement. "Give me a call later. If you would like, in my slow cooker, I have stew cooking that will be ready by supper. Why don't I bring it to your place and we can all have supper together?"

"I love stew," said George as his mouth started salivating. "I will swing by and pick you up at six o'clock. Are you going to be, okay? The redness has faded from your cheeks."

"Yes, I will be fine. Do not worry about me. He just caught me off guard. That will not happen again, ever. I will explain everything to you later tonight. Thanks for rescuing me again."

Harriett giggled at that, remembering when George had rescued her many years before.

He took her hand and kissed it. Then George got out of his car and opened the door for her. He walked her up to her building door. He kissed her once more and watched as she opened the door and went inside. He returned to his car and drove away.

***

That evening as Harriett and George were cleaning up the supper dishes, Scott, who looked exhausted, said, "Thanks for the great supper, Harriett. You make delicious stews. I'm going to lie down now. I will see you later."

"You're welcome, Scott. Have a nice sleep. If I do not see you before I leave, have a good night and I will catch up with you another time."

George and Harriett went into the living room and cuddled on the couch. Harriett finally said, "I want to explain about today, George."

"You do not have to explain anything if you do not want to, Harriett. But I am telling you that if anyone—and I mean anyone—ever hits you or lays a hand on you again, they will wish that they were dead," said George with a hint of controlled anger. He pulled her closer to himself and tucked her under his protective arm. Harriett felt as if she belonged, safe and secure.

"There really is not much to explain, except that it was an error in my judgment. I misjudged who him, and when I finally realized what kind of man he was, I broke it off with him. But he did not take the hint and was making my life miserable. That is why I sold my condo and all my furniture and moved back here. I did not think he would come out here. The thing is, he is a coward, and what you did to him . . . well, he will never come back. Of that, I can assure you. Thanks again for rescuing me."

George turned her face to his and kissed her tenderly. He kissed her cheeks as if to speed her healing. He kissed her eyes and the tip of her nose. Harriett giggled and kissed him back when he found her mouth again.

Chapter 22

Over the next few days, George was busy with new projects. His business was gaining momentum, and he found himself hiring more engineers and support staff. Finally, all past projects that had been put on hold were completed and invoiced. Money was constantly flowing in and flowing out. Yes, business was good.

Scott's hands totally healed, and he returned to work full time. George was ecstatic. He now felt that his whole team was back together, and he looked forward to growing the business. More and more work kept coming, causing the business to operate at full capacity. However, there were still questions to be answered and further safeguards to be put into place to protect the company and the employees.

Rarely was there much time for personal get-togethers. George set up a staff meeting in which everyone was required to attend.

"Good afternoon, everyone. Thank you all for attending this meeting. This coming weekend, the office will be closed. No one is coming in and working. We have all been working so hard, and you deserve a weekend of rest and relaxation. I thank all of you for all your hard work and devotion to bringing this company back from financial ruin.

"On Thursday afternoon, we will have a quick staff meeting, where bonus cheques will be given out to each one of you, after which you can all go home early. The office will be closed Friday, Saturday, Sunday, and Monday. We will open again on Tuesday morning. All our projects are up-to-date, and our new ones can wait until next Tuesday. Are there any questions or concerns?"

"Boss," said Mitchell, "some people have questions regarding our security systems. I would like to address these concerns, if you do not mind."

"Yes, go ahead, Mitchell," agreed George.

"Okay, here goes. What we experienced has taught me more than I thought possible. I know a lot about firewalls, etcetera, but what happened was even beyond my knowledge. I want to assure you that our new firewalls are installed into our system. In fact, let me also assure you that these systems are state-of-the-art. I will not go into detail, because frankly, no one needs to know how these systems work and their security information is vital—only those who work directly with them need this information. In other words, it is a need-to-know situation. Suffice it to say, I assure you that I and Stanley, my assistant, are constantly monitoring and upgrading our systems, keeping them as safe as humanly possible. Should you have any questions or concerns, please come by and see me or Stanley and we will answer your questions the best we can."

"Thank you, Mitchell. Your and Stanley's hard work is very much appreciated. Is there anything else? Yes, Scott?"

Scott stood up to address his fellow workers. He adjusted his tie and ran his fingers through his dark red hair. "I want to take this opportunity to thank everyone for your support during my incapacity. Thank you, Dale, for taking over my project. You did a great job! Good work! I also thank everyone for your concerns and helping me to ease back into work. It is not only the physical that has to heal, but also my mental and emotional state. I was diagnosed with post-traumatic stress disorder. I am not ashamed of my PTSD; it is a fact of my life. But I am healed physically and, with God's help, on my way to full recovery. I thank my Lord and Savior for His unfailing love and healing. Unabashedly, I will be sharing much about the Lord and what He has done for me. I hope that you will allow me the privilege of sharing my testimony with you. Thank you all, and may God bless each and everyone."

All eyes were upon Scott as he sat down. One by one, each person began to clap. Soon, the whole room erupted into applause and cheers for Scott. Scott blushed and lowered his eyes.

"Scott," said George as the noise and clapping abated, "thank you for sharing. It is great what God has done for you. Prayers have been answered. We are all glad that you are back among us permanently.

"If that is all, let us get back to work. Thursday will be here before you know it. Take a pastry and a cup of coffee or juice with you.

Chapter 23

Scott was getting stronger and stronger. His hands were healing, and the physiotherapy was helping him regain flexibility in his fingers. He remembered the Evangelist who saved George. Perhaps it was time for himself to re-evaluate his life and re-dedicate his life to Christ. Picking up his Bible and dusting it off, he opened it to a random page and read:

> *"I am the way, the truth and the life. No one comes to the Father, except through me. (NKJV John 14:6)*
>
> *"Greater love has no one than this, than to lay down one's life for his friends." (NKJV John 15:13)*

Scott began to recall other Scriptures that he had memorized in childhood. The flood of release and freedom of his soul overwhelmed him as tears of cleansing washed over his face and fell onto his chest. Unashamedly, he let the tears flow and peace enveloped him like a warm blanket.

Scott prayed, "Father in heaven, forgive me. I will dedicate my life to You. May Your perfect will be done in my life here on Earth as it is in heaven. Thank you, Lord, in Jesus's name. Amen."

***

The week passed quickly, and George called Scott into his office.

"Hey, Scott," began George, "how was this week?"

"Good, George," replied Scott. "You know a few people have come to see and ask me about my testimony. Isn't that great? I have been able to share Jesus with people."

"That's great, Scott," replied George. "Are you busy tomorrow, any plans?"

"No, I was just going to finish fixing up my condo. Why?"

"Well, I would like you to come over to my place and spend the day together. We have not had a chance to do that for a long time. I am inviting Harriett as well. I will order lunch and dinner. We can talk, play some games—that type of thing. What do you say?"

"Sounds like fun to me. But I am aware of what you want to discuss, George, and I'm ready to tell you everything. I want to thank you for not pushing me. I really appreciate it."

"Oh, that is a relief, Scott! So, I will see you tomorrow morning around eleven?"

"I'll be there," replied Scott. He rose from his chair and shook his brother's hand.

The next day, Scott showed up with a bag full of snacks. He grinned when George looked at him questioningly.

"Can't play games and talk without snacks, right?"

George laughed, took the bag, and placed it on the counter in the kitchen.

"Hi, Scott!" greeted Harriett.

"Hey there, Harriett. How are you?"

"I am fine. I see you are doing well. You look good. How are the hands?"

Scott held up his hands and flexed all ten of his fingers. A big smile lit up his face and brought a twinkle to his brown eyes.

"Is this guy showing off his gorgeous lady-like hands?" teased George as he punched Scott playfully on his shoulder.

"Do you want a coffee, Scott? You, Harriett?"

"Yes, a large strong café-au-lait, please." Scott laughed. "Just black would be great."

"Make mine black too." Harriett laughed as she watched Scott's antics. "You are in a mood, Scott. So nice to see."

"Thank you, my dear. Not many people get a second chance, do they, George?"

Harriett caught a meaningful look pass between George and Scott. She watched them as George set the coffee on the coffee table. Nothing more was said, but Harriett wondered what that look meant. She did not pursue the matter.

Lunch was delivered, and all three laughed and joked while they ate. Once the meal was done, Harriett and George tidied up the kitchen. Harriett poured another cup of coffee for everyone and then sat down next to George on the couch. Small talk ensued as everyone relaxed and enjoyed their after-lunch coffee.

Finally, George said, "Scott, I really need to know and understand why this all has happened to you and to me. When I found you on the floor half-dead, the police found an unsigned letter stating that if I had found it, then you must be dead. Who would've killed you? Why? Why didn't you come to me so that I could help you?"

"Yeah, well, I am ready to talk about it all. But first: the police have been hounding me about all these things. I feigned amnesia until I could speak clearly to them. I wanted to tell you first. You see it all started at university and afterward . . ."

Scott recounted all the things that had happened up to his severe beating.

"I knew who Vince White was . . . what kind of man he was. His viciousness, his hatred of you, his jealousy. He was not the type to forgive and forget. When he was sent here to Crescent River to set up a sleeper cell, he saw you and became obsessed with destroying you. He used the resources that his overseers gave to him, for his own purposes—to destroy you."

George was aghast at hearing Scott's accounting of events.

"I find it hard to believe that a person could be so spiteful and full of hate that they would do such a thing as this!"

"Believe it, George. There are plenty of hateful and evil people in this world; it is sad to say. Vince White was caught up in a web of such evil as the world has not seen to this degree since the days of Noah.

"You have heard of Jacob Weiss. Well, Vince's ambition was to advance up the ranks of his organization the Brotherhood of Theoretical Economics and Political Sciences. Vince was doing extremely well until recently. It is my guess that orders came down from the top to eliminate him. All this investigation was hurting Weiss, and Weiss knew that Vince was using resources for his own purposes. It was costing Weiss millions of dollars and privacy that he could not afford. He has had to withdraw some of his placed people out of here and place the more specialized people somewhere else."

"This is a lot to take in, Scott. I do not understand where you come in and how you know all this stuff."

Scott paused and took a drink of his cooling coffee, thinking about what he was going to reveal and how to say it.

"Scott, George," interrupted Harriett, "I have put on a fresh pot of coffee. I will pour it into the warming decanter and bring it in. Take your time, Scott. I can see that what you must share next is going to cause you some trepidation. Just relax and I will be right back."

Scott gratefully sank back into his chair and closed his eyes, listening to the gentle harp music that George had put on. Telling these things was harder than Scott anticipated, but George deserved the truth—the cold, hard truth.

Harriett came back with the decanter of coffee and a plate of cookies, setting everything on the coffee table. After filling each cup, Harriett sat down again beside George. As if by rehearsal, they each took a sip of hot coffee at the same time.

Scott continued, "These government guys are no joke either. Sometimes, we really wondered who was the worst of the bunch. These guys knew everything about me. Everything about you—about everyone! It is downright scary. When they approached me, I was not really interested in what they wanted me to do. But, oh man, they could make the rain weep with their slick tongues. Finally, they made it sound like it would be in my best interest if I cooperated. Veiled threats, I believe, are their forte. You are my closest friend. . . . No one was off limits to them. So, I did what I had to do. I left as soon as my contract was up with Telstar Engineering and came home. I was informed before I left that Vince White may be coming out here.

"Nothing seemed to be happening here until you were hit. Then I knew that Vince was here for sure. I tried to get to Vince's overseer, which I eventually did. He, of course, was hard to find. These guys also have very deep rabbit holes. Anyways, I finally made contact and explained that you were not who Vince said you were. I explained to him about Vince's hatred of you and that he must be using their resources against you.

"Vince caught wind of what I had done and sent his goons after me, hence—" Scott held up his hands. "I was trying to protect you."

George looked at Harriett, who looked back at George. Both were dumbfounded.

"Why in God's name, Scott, didn't you tell me?"

"Because, you have no idea how hard this is to share. Even now, my telling you could cause you so much grief, could even cost you your life. I am telling you this now because I will be leaving the company. The Lord and I had a long talk together. You see, George, I have re-dedicated my life to God. He is calling me into ministry.

"Where I am going, what my ministry will be, I am not sure yet. We also discussed you. God has assured me that He will look after you, so I do not need to worry about you. And by the looks of it, there is another who will watch your back. A mighty fine looking one at that." Scott smiled at Harriett. "She will take good care of you, my brother. Just wished I could be here for your wedding. Well, who knows, maybe I can."

"Scott, I cannot thank you enough for telling me all these things. I just wished you would have told me sooner. But I do understand. I probably would have done the same thing."

"I think, George, that the threat to this community is over for the present time. But, do be careful and keep your eyes and ears open. Watch your back. Thank you, George, for hearing me out. I really appreciate all you have done for me."

"How long are you going to be here before you leave?" George asked.

"Oh, I will still be here for a while yet. Must get some things worked out, and there are a couple of projects at work that I need to complete. They will take a few months, but I do not want any more projects added to my plate.

"I have been training that new kid, Timothy. He will be taking over for me. He is good, so I will leave my spot in good hands."

Later that afternoon and into the evening, the three played some games, enjoying themselves. All tension was gone, and the talk became light-hearted and entertaining.

Chapter 24

Months passed, and Scott had finished up projects, sold his condo, and was ready to leave Crescent City.

"Tell me again, Scott, where are you going?" asked George.

"I am going to Bible College in the Midwest. I have been taking courses online, and now I am heading out to finish up the first- and second-year exams. I will complete the two years course in one-year and then I will graduate with a degree in Theology and Biblical Studies. I want to bring the Gospel to underprivileged people, concentrating on teaching, especially children. I really like kids.

"You do not know this, but I spent a lot of time at a kids' drop-in center in the inner city. Kids are our future, so giving them a step up in good living and knowing that Jesus loves them will give them the courage to face the future with hope and fortitude. I have already been set up to work with a team going into the jungles of South America. To be exact, I will be going to Uruguay. I will work with the team this summer before school starts. It is a voluntary job right now, but that is okay. Everything will work out."

"I will miss you, buddy. Remember, I will always be here for you. You will do well, Scott. God's favor and His hand is upon you."

Closer than brothers, the two men hugged each other, slapped each other's back, and stepped apart. Scott got into his car and said thickly, "We really are brothers from different parents."

"Right on!" agreed George. He watched as Scott drove out of his life . . . forever? *Who knows where the hand of God will lead any of us.*

Harriett watched the exchange from the kitchen window. She went to the back door in time for George to enter.

"It's always hard on the one being left behind," stated Harriett. She looked into George's sad eyes and, feeling his pain, put her arms around him and hugged him hard. George returned her embrace. He found her soft yielding lips and kissed her with passion and love. All his emotions flowing out and into Harriett's sweet love and grace.

"I love you, Harriett," said George with a deepness of spirit that comes with the true conviction of abiding love. "Will you marry me?"

Harriett took a half step back and looked into his eyes again. She paused a moment, thinking briefly back to the river and seeing him kneeling over her with concern and something else. It was what she was seeing now: love. She smiled.

"Ah, my Georgie, of course, I will marry you. I would have said yes to you when you first asked me when I was seventeen and you were just eighteen. I have waited all these years for this. Yes! Yes! I will marry you. I love you so very much!"

"I will take good care of you, Harriett. We will have a good life. However, there is something that I must tell you, but I just cannot talk about it tonight. I cannot face any more drama. Uh-oh, I see that you may think it is an awful secret. No, it is nothing like that. Really, I will tell you everything in a while. I promise. Let's have a coffee."

Epilogue

Harriett bought shares in George's company, and with her unique talents and skills, she was quickly rising-up the corporate ladder. George would have been happy to bring Harriett into the company as a full partner.

"George," explained Harriett for what seemed the umpteenth time, "I want to progress on my own merits. I do not want a position just because we are engaged. People like me and are responding well to my leadership.

"They respect me because I refuse to take advantage of our relationship. This is important because it will foster good will among all the teams. The company will be known for its fairness, and people will see it as an equal opportunity place of employment. We will draw well-trained and highly motivated people."

"You are right, as usual, Harriett," said George, loving her more and more. "But after we are married next year, you must take your rightful place beside me as a full partner and as vice president. Agreed?"

Harriett nodded her head in agreement. She smiled up at him as he gathered her into his strong arms and gentle hands.

"I love you, Harriett."

"I love you, George, more and more every day. I can hardly wait until I am Mrs. George Hamer. Harriett Hamer goes well, doesn't it, George?"

"Indeed, it does," said George, and he kissed her deeply.

***

One evening, as George and Harriett were sitting in George's living room, relaxing after supper, George said, "Harriett, my love, remember some time ago that I had something to tell you?"

Harriett moved over a little from his side, looked up expectantly into his eyes, and responded, "Yes, I do, George. Are you ready to tell me? I often wondered what it was, but I realized that you would tell me when you were ready."

"I am ready to tell you now. I have never shared this with anyone else, not even Scott, though he was there for me.

"Back in university, you knew that I had been poisoned and had died. I was literally dead. They had removed all the tubes but not the heart monitor, even though there were no signals coming from my heart. They were getting my body ready to go to the morgue. Scott was there, so they left me with him for a while. Well, Scott told me that an Evangelist had ministered to a young boy who died from injuries from a car accident. The Evangelist raised that boy from the dead. Amazing isn't it, how God's Word says that a believer will raise the dead? Anyways, I guess he finished what he was doing and was walking past my cubicle and he asked Scott if he could come in, and Scott agreed.

"He came to the head of the bed. He asked my name. Then he raised his voice and shouted at me to come back in the name of Jesus Christ. I heard it as clear as a bell. His voice carried such authority!"

"Of course, you came back," interjected Harriett.

"Obviously. What I want to share with you is my experience in heaven. Are you ready? This will knock your socks off. Or at least it will amaze you."

Harriett's eyes beamed in anticipation. "Carry on, George, I'm all ears. I have goosebumps down my arms!"

George smiled back at her and chuckled softly before continuing.

"I saw myself and Scott. I tried to tell Scott that I was okay and not to be upset, but he did not seem to hear me. Two very large angels were standing beside me. Each one took my hands, and the next thing I knew, I was standing in a light so bright, brighter than the sun on our brightest day.

"But the light did not blind my eyes. In the center of the light was a man. An extremely handsome man. His clothes shone so very brightly. He walked toward me with a smile that lit up my heart. At least, that was the sensation I felt. Some of this is hard to explain in words.

"The Man, who was Jesus—I knew that instinctively—came closer, and the closer He came, the more His glory shone. Love—love as I have never experienced—enclosed around me like a soft blanket. I felt calm, accepted, and very much loved.

"'George, how nice to see you,' He greeted me. Then He said, 'George, a very grievous thing has happened to you. Come sit here and let us talk.'

"We talked. He showed me heaven. It seemed that we walked and talked for a long time, even though we were sitting down. You should have seen what I saw. There were animals, flowers so big and so beautiful with a fragrance that I cannot adequately describe. Trees . . . huge trees . . . leafy and everything sang.

"Everything sang in harmony. Soft and lightly, everything sang. Birds, colorful and beautiful—they all had their own singing voice as birds do here on Earth, but all these birds sang in harmony. You see, Harriett, there is no discord in heaven. I had a strong sense of business there. I did not see any people, but I sensed their presence. Then, suddenly, I heard a choir. I could not see them. I just heard them. I turned and looked at the Lord. He just smiled and said that they were heaven's great choir getting ready to sing when the saints from Earth come home. Jesus catches all the saints up in a twinkle of an eye, to be ushered into the presence of the Lord God by the choir, welcoming everyone home. Oh, Harriett, it was so very beautiful."

"George," said Harriett softly, taking George's hands into her own, "what did Jesus tell you?"

Regaining his composure, George continued, "Jesus said that it was not my time. He said that the enemy was going to steal, kill, and destroy me. He said that I must go back for He has a plan and a destiny for me.

"Jesus also told me that He wants me in business because He needs, godly, upright people to show the world that the present world system is coming quickly to an end and that businesses operating under the guidelines of the Bible will flourish and will conquer the evil system, known as the Babylonian system. This is in preparation for the millennial reign. For the saints will return with Jesus and rule on Earth for one thousand years. There were other things He told me, but I am not allowed to reveal them. On one thing, though, He did say that the woman I would marry was the one whose life I saved. That, of course, is you. He also told me that we would have a daughter. When she is born, we are to dedicate her to the Lord and to bring her up with love in the admonition of God. We are to guide her carefully in the path of God. It was just then that I heard a voice calling out to me. Jesus then said to me that it was time to go back, for His servant was calling.

"He also gave me His blessing and said, 'Be of good courage, George. Be strong and stay on the path of faith. Trials and tribulations will come, but behold, I have overcome. Go in peace George.' Next thing I knew, I was awake in the hospital. People were excitedly running in and out. But the first person I saw was Scott smiling his goofy smile. How I love that brother of mine! I miss him."

"George, what a beautiful experience! As you were telling it, my spirit was leaping within me. It was as if I was with you. I could plainly see everything you saw. Hear everything you heard. How amazing! Thank you for sharing all of this with me!"

"Harriett, now that I have shared this, we need to find a church that we both agree on and dedicate ourselves to the work of the Lord. What do you say?"

"I say, yes, George! There is a new church that I have heard of just opening here in Crescent River. They are the Word of Faith, which is a break from the Pentecostal denomination. Let us check it out together. We will pray and ask God if this is where He wants us."

"Good idea! Let us start this Sunday."

The following Sunday found George and Harriett at the Free Chapel of Faith. They were warmly greeted by the pastor and his wife. The sermon arose with the message of the Good News. Both

George and Harriett were impressed and touched by the worship and message. They left feeling well fed on the Word of God.

"So, you enjoyed the service, Harriett?'

"Oh yes! I had a sense of complete peace and something stronger in me. I cannot quite put my finger on it. How about you, George?"

While paying attention to his driving, George wanted to shout in happiness. He stopped at a red light. The light changed to green, and George proceeded through the intersection before saying, "I feel the same way as you. I want to raise a hallelujah! God spoke to my spirit, and it is as if I am truly alive!"

George put his hand on Harriett's leg, gave it a gentle squeeze, and said, "It will be you and I, girl, along with Jesus, and we will have a blessed life!"

Harriett shared in his happiness.

Printed in the USA
CPSIA information can be obtained
at www.ICGtesting.com
JSHW082052220823
47040JS00001B/71